WHERE BAD GIRLS GO TO FALL

HOLLY RENEE

Where Bad Girls Go to Fall

Cover Design: Regina Wamba

Editing: Ellie McLove

Stay notified of new releases, sales, and what's happening with Holly Renee:

www.authorhollyrenee.com/subscribe

TO MY FAVORITE BAD GIRL, CASEY.

Baby girl,
There are far too many ordinary people in this world.
Never become one of them.

CHAPTER 1

A PICTURE IS WORTH A THOUSAND WORDS

STACI

I NEVER REALLY GAVE TWO shits about what anyone thought of me.

Did I cuss too much? Fuck yes.

Did I have too many tattoos? That depended on your preference of skin to ink ratio.

Were my nether regions pierced? Only on days that orgasm ends in an M.

I had always been the rebellious girl whose give a damn busted a long ass time ago. I loved adventure and excitement. I would try just about anything once.

Except settling down.

Just the thought of it was giving me hives.

I was a conundrum really. My favorite thing on this entire planet next to orgasms? Romance novels. One of my least favorite things on this entire planet? The idea of spending the rest of my life with one person.

I blamed it on all the romance novels I had read over the years. The heroes were perfect.

Muscles? Check.

Chiseled jaw? Check.

Smooth talker? Check.

Had a job? Check.

Amazing in the sack? Double check.

I just hadn't been able to find someone who fit all those categories. I dated a guy once who may have been the hottest guy I had ever seen, bright blue eyes, covered in ink, and a panty-dropping smile, but he had absolutely no clue what to do once my panties fell.

I could probably find Atlantis before he found my clit.

Then there were all the unrealistic ideas of love at first sight and being one hundred percent sure that he would be the one I was meant to spend my life with.

I mean, come on!

It took me a good ten minutes just to decide what toppings I wanted on my pizza.

I couldn't imagine meeting someone, some magic fucking love dust being sprinkled over my head and thinking "mine." My vagina had that thought sometimes, but not my heart. Definitely not my heart.

But my heart wasn't on my brain at the moment, only my vagina, and how that girl was about to go on strike if I didn't let her visit someone besides my own hand.

I jumped onto my bed and picked up my phone. I ignored the hundred plus emails that were going to remain unchecked, and my finger hovered over my Kindle app before I finally decided to open my contacts.

I scrolled through my phone.

Eric.

Too clingy.

John.

Too small.

Luke.

Too much saliva.

Mark.

Just dirty enough.

I clicked on Mark's name before hitting the small camera icon on the bottom of the screen. Mark was not my happily ever after, but he could easily make me happy for a few hours or so.

He had accomplished that goal several times before.

Laying back in the bed, I positioned myself just right before holding my phone above me and taking the photo.

I looked at the picture of me from my neck down. My breasts were fully on display, the studs of my nipple rings shining in the flash, and I knew that Mark would absolutely love it.

He would know it was me without even having to read my name.

I hit send before throwing my phone down on my bed and heading toward the shower.

If I knew Mark, he would be on his way over here in about fifteen minutes, and I needed to be ready. God, I was so ready.

It had been four weeks and three days since the last time I got laid, but who was counting.

I was.

I was counting the damn minutes.

Because I became a total bitch when I didn't have sex for a long period of time. Even I became annoyed with myself.

I never understood how other women could do it. I had so many friends who felt like they had to be in a relationship to be sexually active with someone, and while I understood their reasoning, I couldn't understand how they could go without enjoying mindless hot sex with someone who you wanted nothing more from.

It was the best kind of sex in my opinion.

No strings attached.

No expectations.

No false declarations of love as you raced to reach your orgasm.

You both knew the score, you both knew the goal, and I was a firm believer in no false promises.

I scrubbed myself down with my loofa before stepping out of the shower and spreading lotion across my skin.

Relationships made you too complacent. They made you too worried about the other person.

I didn't have time to worry about someone else. I had too much going on, on my own. No way did I need to add someone else's shit to the mix.

I just needed them for a few hours, tops.

I wrapped my towel around me and picked up my phone.

Damn, Staci.

Exactly the reaction I was looking for.

You coming over?

I watched as those three little dots danced across my screen.

Where do you live?

What was he talking about? Mark had been to my house a dozen times. He knew his way to my house and around my body.

Stop playing games. I'm wearing nothing but a towel. ;)

Those three little dots only appeared for a second before I got a response.

I'm not playing. Send me your address, and I'll be right there.

I huffed in frustration and ran my hand through my wet hair.

I was about to reply back and tell him to forget it when my

eyes caught the name at the top of the screen, and my heart stopped.

I read it over and over. Praying that my eyes were playing tricks on me.

Mason. Not Mark.

Mason fucking Connor.

I sent a nude photo of myself to Mason fucking Connor.

I sat down on the edge of my bed and tried to breathe through my panic. My fingers gripped my soft sheets so hard that I thought they might rip as I thought about what to do.

I could count on one hand the things I knew about Mason.

1. He was my best friend's brother. Strike one.
2. He was my boss's best friend. Strike two.
3. He was a manwhore. Strike three.

But he was also super fucking hot.

It wasn't that I would have minded his overall manwhoriness in a normal

situation especially with his hotness, but combined with the others, he was one hundred percent off limits.

My finger bounced over the screen of my phone, but I wasn't sure how to respond. How did I explain that my sexting was meant for someone else?

OMG, Mason. I'm so sorry. That was meant for someone else. Please delete that photo.

There. That should take care of it. No harm, no foul.

I'm not.

You're not what?

My heart drummed to the beat of those three fucking dots.

I'm not sorry, and I'm not deleting the photo.

I stared at the screen in disbelief.

Mason!

I was going to kill him.

Staci!

I screamed out in frustration.

Please just delete the photo.

Please just send me your address.

I held the phone in my hand but didn't respond.

I've been hard since the moment you sent it to me. The things I want to do to that body of yours.

I felt my body start to tingle as I read his words and told that bitch to calm the fuck down. We did not want Mason Connor.

There is no way in hell that I am sending you my address.

Nope. It definitely wasn't happening. I may not have been the most wholesome girl around, but I did have standards. And fucking my best friend's brother was one of them.

He just needed to delete the damn photo, and we could forget the whole thing ever happened.

But I should have known that Mason Connor would mess up my plan.

Well, sweetheart. There is no way in hell I'm deleting this photo.

Shit.

I only had two options. I could break into his house, steal his phone, and delete the photo myself, or I could pretend it never happened.

I had a feeling that I was going to regret my opposition to burglary.

CHAPTER 2

THE DEAL

MASON

I SMILED DOWN at my phone before tucking it into my pocket.

Staci fucking Johnson.

I knew she was hot, but I had no idea she had a body like that beneath her clothes. She really wasn't my type either. She was covered in tattoos, her hair was jet black, and her eyes looked like they held more secrets than any one girl should.

But fuck, she was beautiful.

And my dick had been hard as a rock ever since she sent me that picture.

"What are you smiling at?"

I looked up at my best friend, Parker, who I had practically forgotten was sitting across from me before I adjusted my jeans. He took a sip of his beer and narrowed his eyes at me.

"Are you in love?" The words sounded so weird coming out of his mouth.

"What?" I practically choked on my beer. "Hell no. I'm not pussy whipped like you."

It was a low blow, but he was in fact pussy whipped. There was no denying it.

"I'm not ashamed of it." He grinned. "Livy does this thing..."

I held my hand in the air to cut him off. "I swear to God, dude. I know I told you that I was okay with you dating my sister, but I do not want to hear about it." I shuddered and threw back my beer.

"So, you don't want to hear about what she did while I was driving last night?"

"Do you want to die?" I narrowed my eyes at him.

"I was being safe. Ten and two." He held his hands out in front of him to show me his safe driving techniques, and I threw a chip at his head.

"What was that for?" He rubbed his forehead with a shit eating grin on his face.

"Stop talking about my sister like that. Talk to Brandon if you need someone to share with." I looked around the sports bar as I usually would, but not one woman caught my eye. Because Staci had put some sort of voodoo over me. Titty voodoo.

"I'm just busting your balls. Who was the girl on the phone?"

"How do you know it was a girl?" I cocked an eyebrow.

"It's always a girl." He rolled his eyes. "Anyone I know?"

I could have been honest. I mean that man was fucking my sister, but for some reason, I didn't want him to know about Staci. She was his employee and his girlfriend's best friend. My sister's best friend.

It wasn't that he would care. He would be completely fucked in the head if he did, but there was just something about having this little secret with Staci that felt exciting.

She was crazy if she actually thought I would delete that

photo. Just thinking about it now made my dick stir in my pants.

I had been with a lot of women, too many to count really, but I had never seen a woman as sexy as Staci. How had I not realized it until now?

I had been thinking about her ever since she accidentally sent me that photo. At least she claimed it was an accident. All I knew was that it was hot as hell, and I couldn't stop replaying the image over and over in my head.

I thought about it when I was in the shower with my dick in my hand. I thought about it when I was on a date with that chick the other night. What was her name? Fuck. I don't know.

I kept wanting to call her Staci.

I couldn't even bring myself to get laid because all I could think about was Staci.

It was fucking pathetic.

And it was the only thing I could think about as she walked into the bar with my sister. A pair of skintight jeans wrapped around her, but they barely covered any skin through all the rips and tears. Hell, her skin looked so soft underneath.

I wanted to taste every inch of it with my tongue.

It was the thought that was probably running through every guy in the bar's mind as their eyes tracked her as she walked by.

I had the irrational urge to slam their heads into the tables in front of them.

But Staci wasn't my type. She gave off a "Don't fuck with me" vibe with her full sleeves of tattoos, the glimmer of mischief in her eyes, and the sassy attitude she had in spades. I was usually into girls who were much more open in the fuck with me category. I didn't enjoy the chase, and I sure as hell didn't have time to work for it.

Easy, no strings attached fucking.

Staci wasn't easy. She was a wildfire. Fierce and destructive.

I had watched many men pine over her over the years that I had known her, and I had watched each one of them fall flat on their face. Staci didn't date. At least, I never saw her with anyone.

I had never even seen a flicker of interest.

She and my sister hopped on stools at our table, and Staci sat down right next to me. She flicked her hair over her shoulder and her scent hit me. It wasn't the normal flowery perfumes that I was used to. I didn't know how to explain it. She somehow smelled like a hit of fresh air with a bite of something more. Something intoxicating.

Her emerald eyes met mine, and for the first time since I had known her, I saw momentary panic flash before me.

And I ate that shit up.

"Hey, Staci." I smiled around my beer.

"Hey, Mason." Her words were rushed, and she quickly looked away from me to grab the attention of the waitress.

"Two shots of tequila, please, and keep them coming."

"Stressful week?"

Her eyes snapped up to mine and narrowed slightly.

"Something like that."

She spent most of her time ignoring me. Talking to my sister, talking shit to Parker, and downing her tequila shots. But every few minutes, I would catch her eyes on me if only for a moment.

I watched her red lips as they opened to down the shot of liquor, and I stalked her tongue as it caught the moisture on her lips.

"Mason, how's work going?" My sister's voice pulled my attention away from Staci for what seemed like the first time that night.

"Busy. We have a bunch of projects coming up." I took another sip of my beer.

"I drove by that house you've been building on Martin Street. It's insane."

I smiled at my sister. She was right. The house was insane. It was probably one of my favorite projects we had ever done, and it made me proud as hell to have a Connor Construction sign standing firm in the front yard.

"It's pretty cool, huh? You should see the inside."

"Can I?" She looked up at me with her puppy dog eyes that managed to get anything she ever wanted from me her entire life.

"Yeah. Call me one day next week, and I'll show you."

"Awesomesauce." She grinned.

"Did you really just say awesomesauce?" I shook my head at her.

"Yes. What's wrong with awesomesauce? Staci and I say it all the time." She looked to Staci for support.

"I'm not too sure that helps your case."

Staci's eyes quickly turned to mine and a chill ran through me at the spark I saw there. "And why not?"

"Because you're her best friend. You're like two crazy peas in a pod," Parker spoke up beside me.

"Don't you two forget it either." My sister pointed her finger at me and Parker. "We'll fuck you both up if you mess with us."

"Even me?" Parker pointed to his chest.

"Especially you." She grinned.

Parker grabbed her hand and pulled her off her stool and into him. She pretended to put up a fight, but anyone with eyes could see she had no real interest in resisting.

Parker leaned down, whispering something in my sister's ear causing her to blush and me to almost vomit.

"We're going to get out of here." Livy tried to be nonchalant but was anything but.

"What?" Staci shrieked. "It's not even midnight yet."

"I know, but it's been a long week. We're both tired." Livy tucked her hair behind her ear.

"I know you just want to go home and have sex with your man. I don't blame you. Have an orgasm or two for me."

Livy smiled and pulled Staci into her while they both laughed at something Staci was saying in Livy's ear.

"All right man. We're out of here." Parker and I slapped hands. "Wrap it twice." Parker looked around the bar. "It looks like slim pickings tonight."

I chuckled, but I didn't glance to where he was looking. I hadn't paid attention to any other woman in the bar. I couldn't see past her.

"Goodnight." I waved to my sister as her and my best friend walked toward the door.

Staci immediately looked down at her cell phone when we were alone, and it was odd to see this normally one hundred percent confident woman seem a little awkward around me.

"Looks like it's just you and me now, huh?" I rested my chin on my fist and watched her.

"I was actually just leaving." She glanced up at me before tucking her phone into her back pocket.

"Staci leaving before midnight?" I put my hand over my chest in shock. "When did you become such a fuddy dud?"

"I'm not a fuddy dud. I'm just tired." She stared into me, daring me to challenge her.

"Just because I've seen your amazing fucking tits doesn't mean that we can't still be friends."

"Really, Mason?" Her cheeks turned red, and I noted that it was the first time since I knew this fiery girl that I had ever seen her blush. There was something about knowing I was the one to cause it that made me refuse to let her just walk out that door.

"How about a game?"

"A game?" She narrowed her eyes.

I nodded my head.

"What kind of game?" She was twirling a ring around one of her fingers mindlessly.

I put my hands in the air to calm the look on her face. "How about a round of twenty questions?"

"I'm not playing strip twenty questions." She raised an eyebrow, and I chuckled.

"I didn't ask you to. Get your mind out of the gutter."

She started to open her mouth to say something, but I continued.

"But we could make it interesting."

"How so?" She seemed intrigued, and I loved that spark of mischief I saw in her eyes. Daring me to play with her.

"If either of us refuses to answer a question, we have to take a shot."

She thought about it for a split second before she reached her hand out to shake mine. Her inked skin a stark contrast to mine. "Deal."

CHAPTER 3

THE GAME

STACI

"WHO GETS TO GO FIRST?" I asked as I watched him sip his beer.

I didn't think I had ever noticed how amazing his mouth was before, but now I couldn't seem to focus on anything other than the curve of his lips as he traced the beer off with his tongue.

"Well me obviously. It's my game." He grinned, and I ignored the small flip in my stomach. Instead, I waved my hand for him to continue.

"Okay. Question number one." He rubbed his hand over the scruff on his chin as if he was deep in thought. "Did you really send me that photo by accident?"

If I was the kind of girl who blushed, it might have happened in that moment, but I wasn't.

"Yes. It was an accident. I meant to send it to someone else."

"Are you happy..." He started, but I interrupted.

"You had your turn. Now it's mine."

He grinned again, and I rolled my eyes.

He was enjoying this. Far too much.

"Did you delete the photo like I asked you to?" I rested my elbows on the table and leaned toward him.

Instead of answering, he picked up a shot off the table, and I watched the tan skin of his throat bob as he swallowed the liquor.

I narrowed my eyes at him as he wiped his mouth with the back of his hand.

"Are you happy you sent that photo to me and not to whoever it was intended for?" He smirked, a cocky fucking smirk, and I wanted nothing more than to make it drop from his face.

"No," I lied.

"No?" he asked incredulously.

"That's what I said." I leaned back in my chair and crossed my arms. His eyes immediately dropped to my chest, but I didn't dare cover myself. He had already seen it all anyway.

"Why the hell not?"

He shifted in his chair.

"That's more than one question. My turn." I tapped my chin pretending to really concentrate when he interrupted me.

"New rule."

"You can't make up rules as we go along," I huffed. I had a feeling he was used to always getting his way.

"It's my game. I'll do what I want." He rolled the empty shot glass between his fingers. Fingers that were covered in thick calluses from the constant work he did with his hands. "If you lie, you have to kiss me."

"What?" I pulled my attention away from those hands and imagining how they would feel against my skin. "What kind of rule is that? You have no way of knowing if I'm lying or not."

"Yes. I do." He nodded his head.

"How?" I asked, irritated, and I realized that getting under my skin might be one of his specialties.

"A man can't reveal all his secrets."

"And if you lie?"

"I won't, but I'll give you whatever it is you want, Staci."

His eyes were on me, and I tried my hardest to not let him see the shiver that ran through me. Because there was only one thing that was on my mind when it came to him.

What the hell was happening?

I was not into Mason Connor.

"What are we doing here, Mason? Is this about getting revenge on your sister since she's fucking your best friend?"

His eyes sparked with mischief. "If my memory is correct, you are the one who sent me a photo that I haven't stopped thinking about since it flashed across my screen. It's not my fault her best friend is fucking gorgeous."

"So, this is just a game?" I narrowed my eyes.

"Just a game." He smirked, and I knew that look was dangerous. "My turn."

"What's your biggest sexual fantasy?"

At that exact moment, it was getting my hands on him, but I wasn't about to tell him that. Instead, I lied.

"I've already done it."

He watched me for a few seconds before I watched a dimple pop out on his cheek.

"You're lying."

I shook my head at him. "I am not."

"Yes. You are." He leaned back in his chair and lifted his arms behind his head. I watched as his biceps bunched and strained under his t-shirt. "You do this thing with your nose when you lie."

"What thing?" I ran my finger down the bridge of my nose.

"I can't tell you. I'm too busy."

"Busy with what?" He was out of his mind.

"Waiting for you to kiss me." He smirked again, and I decided that it wasn't just dangerous, it was lethal.

And if I wasn't careful, I would fall right into his trap.

I stared at him, thinking about how I should handle him, about how he had somehow managed to make me want to do just that. My legs tightened with just the thought of jumping off my chair and wrapping my arms around him.

But reality came to knock some sense back into me when a petite brunette walked up to his side and wrapped her arm around his shoulders. Shoulders that I was stupidly just thinking about. Shoulders I had no business thinking about, but jealousy still struck me regardless if I had a right to feel it or not.

"Hey, Mason. I didn't know you'd be here tonight."

He looked up at her with a kind smile, and I told myself that I didn't care. Because I didn't. Not really. But there was something about him smiling at her like that that I absolutely hated.

"Yeah. I'm just hanging out with my girl Staci." He nodded toward me, and I rolled my eyes even though some of the jealousy seemed to slip away.

"Oh." She pulled her tan arm off his shoulders and assessed me. Her eyes flicked over me, and I could feel the judgment in her eyes as if she was touching me. She took in my face, she glanced over my hair, and then her eyes dropped down my body to my ratty jeans. The look on her face told me that she had seen everything she needed to, and I wasn't up to par. I couldn't blame her though. I was silently assessing her too. Assessing the kind of girl Mason typically dated. The kind of girl that was the complete opposite of me.

"Yeah. Oh." He laid his hand over his heart dramatically, and I pulled my attention away from her to see him staring at me. "Right before you came over here, we were about to have our first kiss."

"Oh." She took a step back from him and her eyes flitted around the bar. I almost felt sorry for her. Almost.

"It's going to be the most epic first kiss ever."

He winked at me, and I bit the inside of my lip to keep from laughing. His eyes were glued to that lip.

"I'm just going to..." Her voice trailed off as she started walking away from us and the awkward situation he just put her in.

"Why don't we get out of here?" Mason didn't spare her a glance as he spoke to me.

"And go where?" My stomach tensed at the thought, but I wasn't sure if it was from hesitation or excitement.

"Let's grab a bottle of Jack and head down to the lake."

"And our kiss?" I didn't even know why I brought it up.

"No worries, darlin'. You'll get your fucking kiss."

CHAPTER 4

SKINNY DIPPING

MASON

I WATCHED her as she sat down on the dock and dipped her toes in the water. The lake was only about a five-minute drive from the bar, but we didn't talk the whole ride. Instead, she put her feet on my dash and moved them to the music as the wind whipped around her.

I didn't know what I was expecting with Staci, but all I knew was that I wanted to know more.

She kicked her foot causing the dark water to ripple in the moonlight as I sat down beside her. She had rolled her pant legs up her calf, but she didn't seem to care that the water was splashing against the fabric.

"Whose turn is it?" She looked over at me, and for a second, I just stared at how beautiful she was.

"It's mine. I think."

She nodded her head before she turned toward me and crossed her legs Indian style.

"When did you decide you wanted to be a tattoo artist?"

She blinked up at me and furrowed her brow. "A serious question?"

"All my questions are serious." I chuckled.

"I don't know." She shrugged her shoulders. "Forever. I at least knew I wanted to be an artist forever. The tattooing didn't really come along until I figured out..." she hesitated. "Well, until I figured out that your first love isn't always true love."

She said it so matter of factly, like she had put so much thought into what true love was, and I desperately wanted to ask her why. Why wasn't it true love? What happened? But those weren't questions I asked. Those weren't questions I cared about.

"My turn." She grinned, and it was a fake ass grin that didn't do shit to hide the ghosts that were still clouding her eyes. "Where's the craziest place you've ever had sex?"

"Damn. That's a hard question." I rubbed my hand over the back of my neck. "Probably in a movie theater."

"Really?" Staci's laugh rang through the night.

"Yes, really. It wasn't easy, but it can be done. You are looking at a bit of a rebel."

She shook her head and tucked a piece of hair behind her ear.

"Do you want to dance?"

"What?" She laughed again. "No."

"Why not?" I stood from the dock and reached my hand out for her.

"One, we're on a dock in the middle of nowhere. Two, we're probably about to be murdered on said dock in the middle of nowhere." She looked behind her into the pitch-black night. "And three, there is no music."

"I told you I was a rebel." I reached my hand closer for her to take. "Plus, I have this thing called a cell phone that plays music."

She slid her hand into mine as I started the music on my phone.

I pulled her into me as the music broke the calm silence that surrounded us, and her body fit against mine like a glove. She put a hand on my chest, and I was sure it was to keep distance between us.

"Is this how you woo the ladies, Mason Connor? Are you trying to woo me?"

"If I was?" I smiled down at her, and I loved that she barely reached my shoulders.

"Then you would be barking up the wrong tree. I am not so easily won over."

"Oh yeah?" I cocked an eyebrow. "What would it take to win over the elusive Staci Johnson?"

"What was it that you said earlier? I can't reveal all my secrets." She smirked, and my gaze stayed glued to those lips as I fought off the urge to lean down and kiss her.

Instead, I twirled her around in a circle, and she laughed before I pulled her back against my body. We slowly swayed to the beat of the music, and she looked anywhere but at me.

"I have a feeling you don't reveal any of your secrets." I pushed a piece of hair off her face, and she quickly ducked her head away from my touch.

"Have you ever been skinny dipping?"

I wasn't sure if it was the moonlight or my question that lit up her eyes, but either way, I couldn't stop staring at them.

"Actually, I haven't." She looked out over the water, and I followed her stare trying to see what she saw.

"Do you want to?"

The small laugh she let out was infectious, and I found myself pulling my shirt over my head before she could change her mind.

She popped the button on her jeans, and regardless how many times I told myself that Staci and I were nothing more than friends, my dick still went instantly hard.

"Are you going to just stand there and stare at me or are you going to get those pants off?" She shimmied her jeans down her legs, and I picked up the bottle of liquor from the dock and took a swig of the brown liquid to help steady my rapid heartbeat.

The dock rocked under my weight as I kicked off my shoes into the pile of clothes she had started. My pants slid down my legs, and she pulled her top over her head. The smile hadn't left her face since I mentioned the idea, and there was something about it that made me want to dive in head first. Into the water. Into her.

She faced the water and unhooked her bra, and I barely breathed as I watched the delicate fabric slide down her arms. It ran over the intricate ink that covered her body. I had never really paid attention before. Never really thought much about it, but it seemed her skin told a story. A story I was dying to know. A story that begged me to taste every chapter with my tongue.

She looked at me over her shoulder, standing there in nothing but a pair of tiny black panties, and every damn ounce of the alcohol left my body. It seemed that there was nothing clouding my mind at that moment except for her.

I felt sober yet staggering drunk at the same time. Intoxicated on her.

She grinned as she pushed her panties down her legs. Then without a second thought, she jumped headfirst into the pitch-black water, and there wasn't anything in this world that could stop me from following her in.

Chill bumps broke out across my skin as I hit the water, and it still couldn't clear her from my mind. I shook my head as I reached the surface, and there she was. Her dark black hair was pushed back by the water that soaked it and seemed to gleam under the moonlight.

"This feels awesome." She laughed, and the sound pulled me closer to her.

"I cannot believe Staci Johnson has never been skinny dipping before. I'm shocked actually."

"I lived in Oklahoma most of my life. There isn't a lot of skinny dipping where I come from."

She splashed me with water before she ran her hands over her head pushing the excess water out of her face.

"Why did you leave Oklahoma?"

I could see the hesitation in her eyes. The fear that she hid behind her shield. I had crossed the line. I knew before she even opened her mouth that she wasn't going to tell me.

"I guess it's time for another shot, huh?" She laughed, but it was fake and sounded horrible coming from her lips.

"You could always lie to me." I reached out and touched her hand under the water. I was close enough to her that I could easily see her body, but I didn't let my gaze drop from hers.

And I begged her to lie to me.

CHAPTER 5

TEASE

STACI

"YOU COULD ALWAYS LIE TO ME."

His words echoed in my head.

His fingers grazed against mine under the water. I knew what he wanted, and God, I wanted to lie to him. Every ounce of my body was begging me to, but deep down I knew that crossing that line with Mason would be a mistake.

There was nothing in the world that I wanted more in that moment than him, but he was already getting closer than I typically ever let any other guy.

And that scared the shit out of me.

This thing with Mason was just a game—a fun night, a quick fuck.

Why did he have to ask about Oklahoma?

Of all the different questions I had expected to come out of Mason's mouth, he managed to find the one topic that could gut me. The one topic that I refused to think about even to myself.

Because I didn't talk about home.

I didn't talk about the girl I was there.

Because I had left everything about that girl behind. I

couldn't even remember her. The girl who left a trail of tiny fucking pieces of her heart as she ran out of that state before she could change her mind.

Before she ran back to the man who had been crushing her for years.

Just thinking about it made me shudder and made me remember why I had become the woman I now was.

"Just lie to me, Staci." Mason's voice broke through to me, and I stared at him, my entire body begging me to give in, but I was too smart. I had learned my lesson a long ass time ago, and no matter how badly I wanted him, he wasn't worth the risk.

He wasn't worth my heart.

I pulled my fingers away from him and put some distance between us. I couldn't think when he was that close to me. I couldn't fight him off.

"Mason Connor, are you trying to steal a kiss?"

He grinned, the moonlight glittering across his face, and he looked like a wolf that wanted to eat me alive.

"I'm just following the rules of the game, babe." He reached up onto the dock and pulled down the bottle of whiskey before handing it to me. I watched him as I placed the bottle to my lips and let the warm liquor burn my throat. I felt intoxicated just on the taste, and I knew I had to get out of there.

"What do you want to do now?" I handed him back the bottle, and he slammed it against the dock before making his way closer to me. "What are you doing, Mason?" I swam backward, my back hitting the dock, the wood biting against my skin.

"You only get one question, Staci."

"You didn't answer my question." I pointed out.

"Right. I really need a drink right now." He continued moving toward me and my breath raced out to match his pace.

"You just put the bottle on the dock," I said, completely confused, as he reached me, his arm wrapped around my back.

"Well, it looks like I fucking lied."

His deep rattling breath echoed against my cheek, and he gripped my wet hair in his fingers. Then he lowered his mouth to mine, and my heart thundered in my chest. The word stop was on the edge of my lips, but I couldn't get it out. I couldn't do anything as I felt his lips touch mine. It was feather-light, barely a whisper of a kiss, and it was so unexpectedly gentle that my body betrayed me as it arched into him seeking more.

His callused fingers trailed down the arch of my back, and a shiver of pleasure ran through my body.

I wanted more.

It was all I could think about.

All thoughts of self-preservation flew out the window. I didn't care what happened. I just needed him.

I leaned into his kiss, and he retracted an inch.

I huffed out in frustration, and he laughed before he nipped my bottom lip in between his teeth.

I groaned and pushed my body closer to his, and I wrapped my arms around his shoulders as I tried to pull his mouth closer to mine. But his hand in my hair tightened and my legs creeped around his waist. He dropped an infuriatingly gentle kiss to the corner of my mouth before his lips trailed a path down my neck.

His teeth nipped at my skin before he traced the delicious ache with his tongue.

I gripped my own hand in his hair and tried to bring his face back to mine, but Mason didn't let the bite of pain I knew I was causing deter him in the slightest. It only seemed to fuel him, and it drove me fucking crazy.

He used the lake water that trailed down my skin as a map. His tongue followed the rivets as they ran down my skin. He caught the water between his lips before he sucked it off my skin like he was dying of thirst.

My legs tightened around him, my body involuntarily begging him for more, and his hand gripped my thigh holding my center just a breath away from him as his teeth lightly sank down around my collarbone.

"Mason," I cried out his name as I gripped my fingers tighter into his hair.

But he just ate up my cries and continued his torture.

A sweet fucking torture, and I felt too vulnerable.

A vulnerability I didn't allow. A vulnerability that I was incredibly careful to never show, but Mason refused to let me hide.

He refused to let me do anything but hang on to him and take in the pleasure that he was allowing me to have.

And it was infuriating.

I groaned in frustration at having no control or from the fact that he was somehow making me not care. That he was somehow making me want more of whatever he was willing to give me.

Then with an unexpected roughness that made me mad with lust, he sucked on the skin just behind my ear and let his ragged breathing dance against my skin.

The urge to tell him how badly I needed him was on the edge of my lips, but I was silenced when he peppered three excruciatingly gentle kisses against my skin then pulled away from me.

I blinked my eyes open slowly, the moonlight hitting me only moments before the fire in his eyes.

A fire that I knew was staring straight back at him.

I waited for him with my heart thundering in my chest. I waited for his next move, for his next touch, but I didn't expect his hand to graze against my cheek before he pushed some stray hairs out of my face.

He pulled my arm from around his shoulder before he took my hand in his.

"Let's go." His voice was rough and laced with want.

"Where are we going?" I asked as I unwrapped my legs from around his body.

He stared into my eyes for a moment too long to ever be casual. "I want to show you something."

So, I let him guide me out of the water, and for the first time in as long as I could remember, I let him take the lead.

CHAPTER 6

SEDUCTION OR MURDER

MASON

STACI'S HAND rested in mine as I searched for the key on the keyring in the dark. She giggled as I tried two different keys with no luck.

"Are you sure we are supposed to be here?" she whispered before looking around the neighborhood. "I'm not equipped for jail."

"Yes. I'm sure." I gripped another key in my hand and sighed in relief when metal slid upon metal and the lock finally opened.

I pushed the door open and tugged her in behind me.

I watched as she took in the dark space. She ran a hand over the wood covering one wall as her other hand slipped out of mine. She walked toward the kitchen, her fingers flicking the light switch before she turned toward me.

"No lights?" I could barely see her cocked eyebrow.

"No. The electricity won't be turned on until later this week." I pushed off the wall and made my way to her.

"If I didn't know better, I would say that you either brought me here to seduce me or kill me, Mason Connor."

I chuckled as I reached her, and I pinned her against the counter. My body pressed fully against hers.

"Are you sure that you know better?" I ran my nose along the skin of her neck and breathed in her scent.

"Well, I pray that you didn't bring me here to murder me." Her words were breathless, and I knew exactly how she felt.

"Then there is always seduction." I pressed my lips against her neck where I could feel her rapid heartbeat, and I watched chill bumps break out on her skin.

But she wasn't completely correct. I had no damn clue why I brought her here. I just knew that I needed more time with her. I needed more than a quick fuck in the lake.

Because if I let it, that was all we would ever be.

So, I pulled away from her and reached for the flashlight that was sitting on the counter behind her before I clicked it on and illuminated her gorgeous face.

"Would you like the grand tour?"

She smiled at me, a smile that was mixed with lust and something I couldn't quite put my finger on, then she followed me through the house.

"So, you built all this?" She constantly trailed her fingers over different elements of the house. She ran her finger down the wall of the hallway. She rubbed circles with her tattooed finger against the barn wood door that led to the bathroom.

"I mean I didn't do it all by myself, but yeah, my company did."

She sat down on the floor of the master bedroom and I followed her before I balanced the flashlight on the ground.

"It's incredible, Mason." She laid down, her back pressed against the floor as she stared at the ceiling.

"Thank you." My shoulder bumped against hers as I rested my head next to hers.

"You're going to build me a house one day."

She was so sure of her words, and I turned my head to watch her and I could see her ideas practically dancing in her eyes.

"I want a house with a huge wrap around porch because I love to be outside when I draw. And I want a huge kitchen. Not that I cook or anything."

I snorted, and she nudged me with her elbow.

"Why do you need a big kitchen if you don't cook?"

"Because surely someone will cook for me."

I huffed, and she shushed me.

"Stop talking. You're ruining my day-dreaming."

I turned my head back toward the ceiling and tried to hide the smile that was on my face.

"I will have artwork everywhere. I have so many pieces that I've collected that I have nowhere to hang in my apartment, and I'm going to have the biggest damn bathtub you ever saw. I mean huge."

She spread her arms out as far as they would go.

"I will soak in that damn thing every single night."

"Is your manservant going to come in and feed you cheese and grapes as you relax?" I looked at her out of the corner of my eye, and I watched her mouth twitch.

"If I feel like being bothered."

I watched her inked skin as she moved her hand theatrically as she spoke. There was a red watercolor rose on her right forearm that had words bleeding into the ink, but I couldn't make out what it said with such little light. I wasn't sure how I never cared to read what it had said before.

How was I so uninterested?

"I'll make you a deal. I'll build your first house if you give me my first tattoo."

She turned toward me so quickly that I jumped back slightly.

"What are you talking about?" She was on her side, and she had her head resting on her elbow as she stared down at me.

"Which part?" I asked hesitantly.

"You mean to tell me that Parker James is your best fucking friend and you don't have a tattoo?"

"No. I don't have one." I shook my head.

She sat up completely then and lifted my shirt as she went.

"I don't believe you. There is no damn way."

"You just saw me completely naked in the lake. I think you would have noticed if I had a tattoo." But I didn't stop her search.

"I wasn't really looking for tattoos at the time." She pushed against my side to get me to roll over so she could look at my back.

"Distracted?" I asked as I wiggled my eyebrows.

"Please." She rolled her eyes. "I didn't even look down there."

"Sure, you didn't." I chuckled as she rolled me back onto my back.

"Let's go." She climbed to her feet, and I just stared up at her.

"Where are we going?"

"I'm going to give you your first tattoo before you change your mind."

I sat up on my elbows and looked at her like she was crazy. "You've been drinking. There is no way that I'm letting you give me a tattoo tonight."

"Be serious." She crossed her arms over her chest, and even though I tried my hardest not to, my eyes dropped to her breasts. "I haven't had a drink in hours. Plus, you drove me here. Would you have done that if we had been drinking too much?"

"No," I said hesitantly because she was right. I never would have driven her if I was at all impaired.

"Then let's go." She rubbed her hands together, clearly excited.

"Are you sure this is a good idea?" I stood up off the floor and followed her back through the house before looking down at my watch. "It's two thirty in the morning."

"Mason Connor, are you being a fuddy dud?" She arched a perfect black eyebrow at me, and even though I did think going to get a tattoo right now probably was a wild ass idea, I was craving her brand of wild.

"Don't use my own words against me."

She just smiled, and I clicked off the flashlight and followed her out the door.

She spun around in the yard, the only light that of the moon, and I laughed as she danced around in pure bliss.

"You are not going to regret this." She pointed at me as she made her way around my truck and climbed into the passenger seat like she belonged there.

"I'll remember you said that." My truck thundered to a start and my hand grazed her shoulder as I turned to back out of the driveway.

"Don't you trust me?" She batted her eyelashes at me playfully, and I wanted to tell her that I didn't know because the girl in front of me was unlike anything I had ever met. She was different from every other woman.

She was wild, she was real, and even though I did want to fuck the shit out of her, I was genuinely having fun just being around her and that scared the shit out of me.

CHAPTER 7

THE TATTOO

STACI

I PUSHED him back in the tattoo chair and stifled my laugh as he huffed.

"I swear it's not going to be that bad." My fingers slid into my black gloves, and he watched every move I made.

I poured ink. He watched every drop of every color.

I hooked up my gun, and his eyes jumped to my hands when it began buzzing.

"I swear to God if you tattoo a penis on me, I will murder you."

The snort that left me was beyond unattractive and also beyond my control. "I hadn't thought of that actually, but thank you for the idea."

He rolled his eyes and leaned his head back against the headrest.

"It's bad enough that I'm letting you give me my first tattoo in the middle of the night in an abandoned tattoo shop, but letting you decide what to give me..." He shook his head. "This is a bad fucking idea."

"Live a little, Mason. I had taken you for the adventurous, adrenaline junkie type."

His eyes turned to meet mine. "There's a difference between jumping out of a plane and getting something permanently marked on your body that you aren't even seeing first."

I just smiled at him because even though he looked scared to death that I might actually tattoo an appendage on him, I knew he was going to love the actual design.

"Take off your shirt."

He groaned again but leaned forward and pulled his shirt over his head. I just stared. Because even though I had just seen him shirtless in the lake, Mason had a body that took your breath away no matter how many times you looked at it. And under the bright lights of the shop? Holy shit. It was really unfair how perfect every little line and ridge of his body was. He either worked out a ton, or he really worked his ass off when he was at work.

And I was going to put my artwork on his perfect, unmarred body.

Just the thought had a chill running down my spine.

"Okay. Don't look." I gripped the drawing that I had been working on for the last hour in my hands and slowly pressed it against his ribs where he said he wanted it. His eyes were focused on the ceiling, and I pressed the contact paper firmly against his skin before I slowly peeled it away.

I had him sit up and twist this way and that way before I decided it was in the perfect place. Then I dipped my gun into the blue ink and looked up at him.

"Are you sure you're ready?"

He blew out a deep breath and looked back up at the ceiling.

"Yup," he said the word so quickly. "Let's do this shit."

I touched the gun to his skin and made my first mark, and he didn't move an inch. I wasn't even sure he was breathing.

But I fell into a rhythm. My music echoed off the dark magenta walls of my space, and I sang the words in my head as I focused on my art.

It was typically so easy for me to get lost in it, to get lost in the one thing I loved more than anything else, but every time Mason moved slightly under my hands or made a noise, I was acutely aware of my hands on his body.

I wiped off the excess ink with a paper towel before I tossed it into the trashcan at my side.

"That's a lot of blue."

Mason's words caused me to look up at him. "You don't like blue?"

"I love blue." He grinned but still didn't look down at where I worked.

I had asked him on the ride over here what were three things that he loved. Three things that meant more to him than anything else. His answers were simple.

Family, his career, and the mountains.

And as soon as he said it, my mind took off.

I knew that I would do a mountain scene on him, but not just some boring old mountain scene. Mason was far from boring or ordinary and his tattoo had to match.

So, I bent over my drawing table and sketched the sharp lines of the mountains. I penciled in and erased the geometric triangular shape that encased it. Then I envisioned the shades of blues and purples I would use to make the wild watercolor night sky that bled down into the mountains.

The blues and purples bled together as I continued my work, and the colors looked so damn good against his tan skin. It was like the colors were mixed with him specifically in mind.

"Now purple, I'm not too sure about." He chuckled as I tossed another paper towel in the trash.

"Shh." I didn't even look up at him. "You're messing up my concentration."

He was, but it wasn't his words. It was the way his abs bunched as he slowly breathed in and out, it was the way his arm would tense slightly as I hit a particularly sensitive spot with my tattoo gun, and it was his scent that I had smelled all night. But not this close. When I was this close to him for this damn long, it was intoxicating.

And there was something about him trusting me enough to let me design a tattoo and ink it on his body that was even more intoxicating.

It was fucking with my head.

"It's done." I glanced up at him as I wiped the excess ink off his skin again, and he was staring at me. Not at where my hands worked against his body, but at me. His gaze roamed over my hair, my face, and the ink that marked my own skin.

"Yeah?" He stretched out his arm that had been in the same position for the last hour or so and moved it around.

"Do you want to see it?" I pulled my gloves from my hands and tossed them in the trash as I tried to hide my smile. Because regardless of what he thought, I loved it. I just hoped he loved it as much as I did. I hope it actually fit him as much as I felt it did.

He sat up in the chair and looked over at me again before he took a deep breath and faced the full-length mirror in the corner of the room.

My breath caught in my throat as I watched him take it in. He stared at the art, his gaze flicking to detail after detail, and when his eyes met mine in the mirror, I let out the breath I had been holding and I smiled.

CHAPTER 8

CAUGHT

MASON

I DIDN'T HAVE a clue what to say to her.

I just stared at the tattoo in astonishment.

How the fuck did she do that? I didn't even have an idea of what kind of tattoo I wanted. That's why I had a best friend who was one of the best tattoo artists in the business but no tattoo. He had asked me so many times over the years to give me one. Actually, he was probably going to be pissed as hell when he saw that I let Staci do it.

But it was perfect.

Every line. Every detail. It was like she knew exactly what I wanted without me even knowing.

The colors of the night sky were vibrant against my skin and a stark contrast to the sharp lines of the mountains.

I lifted my arm and turned more to my side. It was like it was made to be on my skin. As if I couldn't even remember what my body had looked like before it was there.

I looked up at her in the mirror. She was standing behind me smiling, and I knew that she knew how perfect it was without me even having to say words. But I had still planned on saying them. I planned on telling her how much I loved it. How perfect it was. How perfect she was. But when I turned to face her, none of that came out of my mouth.

Nothing did. Because I couldn't think beyond the fact that I was dying to kiss her. The urge overwhelming.

I stalked toward her, and her pupils dilated as I came closer and closer to her. She opened her mouth to say something, but I didn't give her a chance.

I ran my fingers in her hair, and I slammed her small body back against the wall as my body pressed fully against hers.

She moaned, soft and low, and I swallowed the sound when my mouth met hers.

It wasn't the same kind of kiss as earlier.

That kiss was slow, calculated, teasing.

That kiss was from the guy who was smooth with the ladies.

But this kiss?

I didn't even know what the hell this kiss was. All I knew was that I had lost every bit of control that I normally possessed, and I was dying to taste her. I was dying to taste every single part of her that she would let me.

She moaned again, and my tongue slipped inside her mouth. Her tongue touched mine, and I needed more. I gripped her thighs in my hands, trying to gain some ounce of control, but that flew out the window when she lifted her legs and let me pull them around my hips. I pressed my body farther against hers, and we moaned in unison as our centers pressed against one another.

Staci seemed to possess as much control as I did. She gripped my hair in her hands, and she tugged at the strands causing a bite of pain as she nipped at my lip. She ground her hips against me, and I shuddered as I felt her tight little body against mine.

I lifted her from against the wall, and I didn't even think as I slammed her down against her worktop. Shit flew everywhere.

Ink of every different color that she had painted onto my body dripped to the floor, down our legs, but neither one of us cared.

Staci reached between us and gripped the edge of her shirt in her hands before it went flying through the room. My mouth instantly dropped to her chest. My kisses a frenzy of lips and tongue and teeth against her soft skin. Her perfect breasts were still encased in her tiny black lace bra, but I didn't let it deter me.

I latched my mouth around the lace. She leaned her head back on a silent cry, and something else hit the floor as her hands reached out for something to ground her.

I pressed my lips gently against her sternum before I hooked my fingers into the front of her bra and roughly jerked the fabric down her body.

"Oh God." Her words hit me just as my mouth pressed against her nipple for the first time, and I groaned as she pressed her body farther against me. She had an intricate tattoo that ran from the bottom of her sternum to under her breasts, and I felt mesmerized as I traced the design with my tongue. Staci bucked against me, and I bit down on the skin above her ribs as I popped the button of her jeans with my fingers.

Her hands frantically reached out for me, desperately trying to find my own jeans, and I chuckled softly when she growled her frustration.

I leaned back from her long enough to unbutton my jeans and pull down the zipper, and I watched as she raised her hips from the small table where she sat and pulled her jeans and panties down her body.

I barely managed to push my own jeans six inches down

my hips before she hooked her heels behind my body and pulled me back into her.

She was so fucking wet against me, and any chance of being gentle with her, of taking my time, was demolished.

She ground her hips against me using her legs that were wrapped around my back as leverage. My hand gripped the edge of the table to help hold me steady and my fingers became coated in wet ink that still dripped to the floor.

Staci peppered kisses against my neck. She nipped my skin before stroking it with her tongue, and I felt like I was going to combust before I even got inside her.

I couldn't wait any longer. I couldn't stand not feeling her completely around me.

My fingers trailed against the skin of her inner thighs, eliciting a deep moan from her, and I lined my cock up against her. She didn't even give me a moment to move. Didn't even give me a chance. She lifted her hips from the table and pushed her body down around me before I could even think straight.

Fuck. She was driving me crazy.

My hands gripped her ass, and I pushed into her hard. Her fingers clung to my shoulders as I slammed into her again and again. My breath rushed out against her neck, and I ran my tongue against the skin there and tasted the light sheen of sweat.

Her soft moan only fueled me. Pushed me beyond the small thread of control I was clinging to.

I lifted her from the table, and her mouth met mine as I blindly carried her to the tattoo chair I had just spent the last hour in. My ass hit the chair and her knees settled on either side of me as I leaned back.

She pushed against my chest, pushing her up to where she stared down at me, and I watched as I let her take control.

Her eyes were glazed over with lust, and I loved that she

had no makeup on her face. It had been washed off by the lake water that also washed away the thin line we were trying not to cross. A line that had been obliterated.

She used her knees to slowly lift herself up and her eyes never left mine as she lowered herself back down on me at a torturous pace. Her nails raked down my chest bringing a growl from me that I had no chance to keep in, and it seemed to fuel her. She rose back up and dropped down so quickly. I gripped my fingers on her hips. Feeling her hips move against me. Feeling them take every ounce of my pleasure.

There was shock on her face when I used my hands on her hips to lift her, and she groaned as I easily turned her away from me and lowered her on me once again.

One hand caressed her breast, and she leaned her back against my chest as she arched into my touch. My other hand ran along the length of her body before she jumped at the touch of my fingers against her clit, but I didn't give her time to take another breath as I circled my tongue against her neck to the same rhythm as my fingers.

"Fuck." Her moan was long and rough, and she moved quicker and quicker against me.

I slammed into her and her body tensed around me as her pussy tightened.

"Hello?" Brandon's voice called out, and I only thought her body had tensed above me before.

"What the fuck?" she whispered as she tried to move off me, but I kept my hands steady against her and held her in place.

The door to her tattoo room was closed, but there was no lock on the door. No lock to keep Brandon from walking in at any moment.

"Staci?"

Staci glared at me over her shoulder when she tried to get

up again and I refused to let her. Instead, I leaned into her and nipped her earlobe before whispering, "You're not going anywhere." I thrust up into her to drive my point home.

"Who the hell is already here?" Brandon's voice came closer to her door, and she tensed even further as I began thrumming my fingers against her clit.

Her head slammed back against my shoulder, and she clamped her hand down over her mouth to stifle her moan.

"You should probably say something so he doesn't come in here," I whispered to her without slowing down in the slightest.

She nodded her head against me and I watched her throat bob as she tried to calm herself down.

"It's me, Brandon," she called out. She barely managed to get his name out of her mouth as I thrust into her harder and harder. There was something about hearing his name leave her lips while I was inside her that made jealousy spark inside me.

"What are you doing in there?" Brandon said from just outside the door and his knuckles softly rapped against the door.

I rolled her small nipple ring between my fingers and bit down on her shoulder. Her hips rolled against me, begging me for more.

"Answer him," I growled in her ear, and she whimpered as she continued to move her hips to meet mine.

"I'll be out..." I slapped her clit softly, and she bit down on her lip. "I'll be out in a minute. Just give me a few."

As soon as the words left her, I slammed into her again and again. She turned her mouth into my neck, and her breath crashed into my skin.

"Oh, God. Oh, fuck." Her fingers wrapped in my hair. "Mason, please."

I pushed the palm of my hand against her clit piercing and

ground her into every hard inch of me as she fell apart around me.

Her body shook, and I thrust into her one last time as I found my own release.

Our bodies were covered in sweat, her floor was covered in ink, and everything that once sat on her work table was now thrown around the room. And for the first time that night, I realized that the girl who was on top of me, the girl who I was still inside, had not only branded me with her art and her ink, but somehow, the fiery girl who wasn't my type had managed to brand herself somewhere far deeper.

CHAPTER 9

HOW MANY INCHES?

STACI

"OH, FUCK." Oh, God. "What were we thinking?" This was crazy. I paced around my wrecked room and gripped my hair in my hands.

"Calm down." His voice was gruff as he buttoned his jeans, and I was momentarily distracted by the deep V of muscles that disappeared into those jeans like a map. I was in so much trouble.

"Calm down? Calm down? I just fucked my best friend's brother. How am I supposed to calm down?"

He just smirked at me, and even though the damn curve of his lips made my thighs tighten involuntarily, I wanted to kill him for how calm he was.

"You have to get out of here before everyone sees you." I looked up at the little clock on the wall and cringed. How in the hell had we managed to spend the entire night together when it had only felt like minutes? "Your sister and Parker will be here in an hour."

He pulled his t-shirt down over his shoulders, and I winced when I saw his tattoo. I hadn't cleaned it. I hadn't wrapped it.

Instead, I just got on top of him and rode him like I had lost my damn mind.

"Hold on." I slid gloves onto my hands before grabbing more supplies out of my drawers. He let me lift his shirt, and he only winced slightly when I squirted the cold solution against his skin. He watched me intently as I covered his tattoo and pressed the tape against his skin.

"Here are the care instructions for your tattoo." I handed him a little card that had all the instructions. "Make sure that you..."

"I'll leave on one condition."

My eyes jerked up to his. "What condition?"

"Kiss me."

God, I watched his lips as he said the words, and there was nothing in the world that I wanted to do more. But that was why this wasn't a good idea. He had to know. He had to see the damn line we were crossing.

"This isn't a good idea, Mason."

"I think it's a little late for that. Don't you think?"

I shook my head so I would stop staring at his mouth. A mouth that was surrounded by his scruffy beard. A mouth that I had no business looking at and sure as hell had no business kissing. "I don't date."

"Great." He pulled his boots onto his feet, and I realized I was still standing there in my bra. "Neither do I."

His grin was so heady that I knew I would easily become lost if I wasn't careful.

I pulled my shirt over my head and stepped into my jeans. My panties were nowhere to be seen.

"I'm not going to be your fuck buddy."

He watched me as he leaned against the wall. "Fine. Then we can just be buddies."

"Buddies." I rolled my eyes as I slipped my feet into my shoes.

"Yeah. You know? Friends." His eyes were twinkling, and even though I knew how bad of an idea this was, my blood heated at the mischief that sparked in his eyes.

"Friends sure as hell don't kiss each other."

"You're right." He nodded his head slowly. "Just give me one last kiss then we shall enter the friend-zone that is impossible to escape."

I took a tentative step toward him and his grin only widened.

"One more kiss."

He watched every step that brought me closer to him. "That's all I'm asking."

"Then this little game that we've been playing is over."

"Done." He reached his hands out and gripped mine as he jerked my body roughly into his. My core tightened and he knew. He knew exactly what he was doing to me.

He dipped his head low, and he ran his nose along the skin of my neck. Chill bumps broke out across my skin. His bottom lip touched the edge of my earlobe, and I bit down on my own lip because I refused to give him even one more whimper.

"I won. You know?" His teeth bit down on my earlobe.

"You ass." I pushed my hands against his chest to get away from him, but he wasn't having any of it. Instead, his fingers slid to my jaw, tipping my face back so I had no choice but to look up at him.

His smirk was gone from his face as he stared down at me. As he looked over every inch of my face like he was trying to memorize this moment, memorize me. He pressed his thumb against my bottom lip dragging it down as he watched the movement then his mouth devoured mine.

It didn't matter that it was a goodbye kiss. That it was our last kiss.

It somehow fueled me more than any kiss that we had shared all night. Somehow it tore into every part of me. Every part of me screamed to not let him leave.

But I knew that none of that was logical.

I wasn't this girl. I wasn't the hopeless romantic who got butterflies from a one-night stand.

But as soon as I thought the words, my chest ached. I had plenty of one-night stands in my life. This didn't feel like that. Even if it was completely foolish to think it, this felt like something more.

He gripped my hair in his hand and pulled my head back so I was completely open to him as he devoured my mouth.

And when he pulled away, I instantly felt his loss.

I wasn't even sure who I was as I lifted my fingers to my mouth and ran them over the tingle that still lingered there.

He looked as completely dazed as I did. Lost in whatever the fuck this was.

But we were running out of time.

I walked past him and opened the door. The shop was empty with no signs of Brandon to be seen. I took a deep breath before I turned back to face him again, and I schooled my features. I became the Staci that I allowed everyone to see, not the fool that I had somehow let slip only moments ago.

"The coast is clear." I grinned at him. "Remember," I pointed my finger at him, "this stays between us."

He saluted me and I rolled my eyes.

He walked out of the room, and his fingers trailed against mine as he passed me. I clamped my eyes shut to shut down the feelings that were whirling through my head. The feelings that he couldn't seem to leave alone.

He took five steps through the shop before he turned back

to face me. He opened his mouth, to say what I will never know because a throat cleared behind us and I winced at the sound.

Mason and I both turned to look at Brandon as he leaned against the counter with a shit eating grin on his face.

"Hello there," Brandon said as his eyes bounced between me and Mason.

"Hey, Brandon." Mason couldn't hide his small smile, and when I narrowed my eyes at him, he just shrugged his shoulders. "Have a good day."

"You too." Brandon looked down at a piece of paper in his hands. "Although, it seems like it's already off to a great start."

A chuckle burst out of Mason and I looked to the ceiling and prayed for something to save or smite me down. It didn't really matter as long as I didn't have to stand here and endure these two. But my view was blocked when Mason stepped up to me and looked down at me with a soft smile on his face. A different smile than the usually cocky look that it usually held.

"Thank you for my tattoo. I love it."

I nodded my head because I didn't trust my voice. I could barely think right now let alone speak. He leaned down and pressed his lips softly against my cheek, and I closed my eyes as his skin touched mine. The kiss was gentle, but he lingered. Then he was gone.

The door clicked behind him as he walked out of the shop, and I blinked my eyes open. I tried to let reality to sink into me, to ground me, but I could still feel his lips on my skin. I could still feel him over every inch of my body.

"Do you want to explain to me why Mason Connor was leaving your tattoo room at seven o'clock in the morning?"

I looked up at Brandon and just like that, reality hit me like a ton of bricks. I turned away from him and headed back into my room, but I heard his footsteps trailing me.

"Mason Playboy Connor. Mason Love Them and Leave

Them Connor." His voice carried into the room, and I braced my hand on my tattoo chair to try to block out his words. "Mason Livy's Going to Flip Her Shit Connor."

"I get it, Brandon." I pulled the rubber band from my hair and shook my hair out before piling it back on top of my head.

"Holy shit." He let out a low whistle.

I turned to look at him, but his eyes were moving around my space. My space that looked like a tornado had gone off.

"That ink is probably going to stain." He pointed to where tattoo ink dripped down my work table onto the floor.

"Are you going to keep giving me shit or are you going to help me?" I bent down to the floor and started picking up all my stuff as I winced. My tattoo gun was lying on the floor along with almost everything else.

Brandon squatted down beside me and started grabbing things from the floor and putting them on my table. Brandon was almost never serious, but he was one of my best friends. I knew that no matter how much shit he gave me, I could trust him.

"So, last night?"

"Really Brandon? Can we just let this go?" I wiped paper towels over the spilled ink and it only seemed to make it spread further.

"Probably not." He took the soiled paper towels out of my hands and handed me more. "Are you going to tell Livy?"

"I don't know." I started to run my fingers through my hair before I realized they were covered in ink.

"Go home." Brandon grabbed more paper towels from my hands. "Your first appointment isn't until this afternoon. Clean yourself up and get some rest."

"I can't." I motioned around the room.

"I'll clean up your fuck fest."

"Seriously, Brandon?" I laughed because only I would get myself into this situation.

"Go." He grabbed the paper towels from my hands and I rested my elbows on my knees.

"I'm fucked. Aren't I?" I didn't just mean with Livy, and somehow, I think Brandon knew that because despite what Brandon liked to show people, he was far more sensitive then he let on. We were the same in that aspect.

"I would say so." He leaned back behind my tattoo chair and scooped something off the floor before he dangled my panties in front of me. "But it looks like you had fun."

...

I had no idea what the hell I was doing.

I stared at my station as I reorganized it for the thirtieth time in ten minutes. My appointment would be arriving any minute now, and I couldn't wait to have a needle in my hand to help numb my mind.

Because all that was currently running through it was Mason and what the hell I was going to say to his sister. To my best friend.

I went home when Brandon had told me to.

I had scrubbed the ink and lake water off my skin, but when a hint of Mason's scent hit me, my hand paused. I didn't want to wash it away.

I laid in the bed and I tried to sleep, but there wasn't a chance. I tossed and turned and thought about what Mason and I had done. I thought about the way his skin felt against mine. I smiled when I pictured his tattoo and how he had given such blind trust in me.

But then the thoughts of how I was going to face Livy

flooded me, and I hadn't been able to think about anything ever since.

And I had somehow managed to avoid her all day.

I couldn't tell her that I had the best night of my life last night with her brother.

Regardless of whether I knew what it was or not.

I couldn't tell her that we had a one-night stand, and I definitely couldn't tell her that I wanted a relationship with him.

Because I didn't.

I knew how they ended.

I could read about love in my romance novels all day long, because at the end of the day, that's all they were, novels. The author got to choose how she wanted their love story to end. She got to handpick their happily ever after and scribble it across the pages that made us fall in as deeply in love as her characters.

I didn't get to chapter thirty when everything was finally back in order and everything seemed to be going perfectly and find out that hero never really loved the heroine at all. He was using her the entire time until he decided he didn't need her anymore.

What kind of love story was that?

Spoiler alert: It fucking sucked.

"What are we doing for lunch?"

I dropped the stack of paper towels I had been tearing off and stacking perfectly as Livy plopped in my chair and scared the crap out of me.

"What?" I turned my eyes to her before dropping to my knees and collected all the paper towels that were now trash. There was still a trace of ink on the floor, and I winced and hoped she didn't see it.

"What's up with you today?" She narrowed her eyes at me and my stomach flipped.

"Nothing's wrong with me." Nope. Not a thing. I didn't sleep with your brother last night.

"I'm your best friend." She looked me up and down. "I know when something is wrong with you. Did you get laid after I left last night?"

Oh. Dear. God.

I couldn't do this. Not today.

"Yeah. That's it." I smiled, but she didn't look convinced.

"Not buying it. Usually, you'd be in here telling me how many inches he was packing, how many times he made you orgasm or what crazy position he put you in. Did he put you in a position that threw your equilibrium off or something?"

Oh, he definitely did that, but it wasn't from some acrobatic sexual position.

"No. I'm just tired. Long night." I stood up from the ground and stuffed the wasted paper towels in the trash.

"I don't believe you. How long was it? Six inches? Twelve?"

I shook my head and looked to the ceiling.

"I'm not having this conversation with you."

"Why not?" She grinned. "Does he have you sprung? Are you about to break out in song about how amazing his dick was?" She giggled to herself and I cringed.

"Please stop."

"Why?" She wagged her eyebrows. "Was it too much for you?"

"For the love of God, please stop."

"I bet you weren't saying that last night." She slapped her knee like the total dork she was as she laughed at her own jokes, and I couldn't take anymore.

"It was your brother."

I wasn't quite sure why I yelled it at her, but I did. I yelled. And she looked like a deer in head lights. She just stared at me, stock still, then she busted out laughing.

"Livy." I tried to get her attention, but she was bent at the waist laughing so hard that she couldn't catch her breath.

"I don't understand what's so funny." I crossed my arms over my chest and stared at her.

"You." Laugh. "Slept." Gasp of breath. "With Mason." More laughter.

"I'm aware of that fact, but what's so funny."

She put her hand on her stomach and tried to calm herself down.

"Was it good?"

"What?" I screeched. "I'm not talking to you about your brother." I ran my hands through my hair that I wished I hadn't washed so it would still smell like him.

"Did you all make plans to hang out again?" She was watching me closely, calculating but still had a large smile on her face.

"Of course not. Mason and I aren't the kind of people who makes plans to hang out again."

"Did he say that or you?"

"What does it matter?"

"It matters." She nodded her head as if that somehow made it true.

"He asked if we could be friends."

"Friends?" She looked down at her lap like she was trying to figure out what was going on. "My brother asked you to be friends?"

"Yes. I don't understand why that's such a big deal." I started tearing more paper towels.

"You are so screwed." She was still laughing, but I turned my attention to her.

"Why?"

"Because I have known Mason my entire life, obviously, and I have never once known him to ask a girl to be his friend."

"Don't be crazy." I waved her off, but my stomach formed a knot. "I'm sure your brother has had plenty of female friends before."

"No." She shook her head. "Not really and definitely not after he's fucked them."

"Can you not talk about your brother"—I looked up at the ceiling—"fucking me?"

"Fine." She stood from the chair and crossed her arms as she looked at me. "So, you and Mason are friends."

"Yes, Livy. Just friends. But you're not mad."

"Of course, I'm not mad."

"How come?" I never thought she would be this calm.

I watched as her dimples popped out. "Because this is going to be fun to watch."

CHAPTER 10

BOYS NIGHT

MASON

INVITING Staci out for a night with the boys might not have been my brightest idea, but I knew she would never agree to come out with me alone. She had agreed to this friendship, but she wasn't stupid.

"So, is this Staci chick hot?" Drew asked before taking a sip of his beer.

Drew and I had been friends since we started working construction together when we were eighteen years old, and when I decided to open my own company, he was the first man I wanted on my team.

"She's hot as hell." It wasn't a lie. Staci was incredibly hot, but she was so much more than that. She was fucking beautiful. "But she's off limits."

"I thought you said the two of you were just friends?" He smirked.

"We are just friends. For now." Another one of my brilliant ideas, but the idea of Staci just shutting me out after the night we had together completely fucked with my head. I didn't do second dates or second hookups, whatever you wanted to call it.

I sure as hell didn't develop friendships based off one night of the best sex I had ever had in my life, but something with Staci was different. It may have made me a pussy, but I would take time with her however I could get it.

"Are you whipped?" my other buddy, Nate, said from the pool table next to us.

"That's a lot coming from you. What time did your wife say you had to be home?" I looked down at my watch, but not before I saw him flipping me off.

"You laugh now, but you should see this thing she can do with her tongue."

I held up my hands for him to stop after I almost spewed my beer. "Don't you try to fuck up the angelic image I have of Macy in my mind." We gave Nate shit about being wrapped around his wife's little finger all the time, but in reality, that motherfucker got so lucky. Macy was a damn catch, and he was right to thank his lucky stars he had her.

"Holy shit." Drew let out a low whistle, and I turned my attention to the door where he was staring.

Holy shit was right.

Staci was standing in the doorway looking around the crowded bar. She was wearing a tiny pair of shorts so short her front pockets hung below the hem and a black tank top that put her tattoos on full display. So damn gorgeous.

"Don't embarrass me, assholes."

I quickly finished off my beer before making my way to her. She was still scanning the crowd, but when her eyes hit mine, she smiled.

And that fucking smile clouded my mind far more than any alcohol I had drunk even dreamed of.

"You came." I wrapped my arms around her tiny frame and pulled her into me.

"Of course I came. I told you I would."

She wrapped her arms around me, but I could feel the hesitation in her touch. When I finally let her out of my hold, she straightened her shirt and looked around the bar.

"Do you actually have other friends or was that just a ploy to get me here?"

I put my hand over my heart as if she had wounded me. "You think so little of me?"

She shrugged her shoulders and a playful smile pulled across her cherry red lips.

I placed my hand on the small of her back and led her to our table toward the back of the bar. Drew and Nate were both sitting at the table, and I rolled my eyes at the matching shit-eating grins on their faces.

I pulled out a chair for Staci. "Guys, this is Staci. Staci, that is Nate and that is Drew."

"Nice to meet you both."

"You too," Nate said as Drew nodded his head in unison.

I was a bit worried that things would get awkward since they didn't know each other, but I should have had more faith in Staci.

She held her hand up against the side of her face so I couldn't see her mouth, but she didn't quiet her words. "I'm actually glad to see you're both real. I was a little worried that Mason was luring me to my death or something. I wasn't quite sure he really had any friends."

"He's actually paying us to be here to impress you." Nate smirked at me, "But he really should have hired some less attractive friends so he could have looked better, ya know?"

Staci looked around the table then her eyes settled on me. "I see what you mean. It does make him lose his allure somehow."

"Okay. That's enough, assholes." I poked her in her side, and she laughed as the server came to our table.

"I'll take tequila on the rocks." Staci pulled out her card, but I pushed her hand back toward her lap.

"Just put it on mine." I looked up at the server who had been giving me fuck me eyes since we walked in the place.

"No way." Staci jerked her hand away from mine to hold her card up again. "I'm paying for my own drinks."

"No. You're not." I shook my head calmly when she looked anything but.

"Mason, I swear to God."

I just ignored her and winked at the server before she walked away.

She narrowed her eyes at the retreating waitress then turned her glare to me.

"We need to set some ground rules."

"Ground rules?" I could see my buddies watching me, both with grins on their faces.

"Yes. Ground rules of our friendship."

"And what would these ground rules be exactly?"

"Well, for one, no paying for my stuff. I'm a grown ass woman."

"Uh huh." I took a slow sip of my beer as I watched her tuck a piece of hair behind her ear. "And the second?"

"I'll have to think about it." She crossed her arms over her chest and looked around the bar.

"What about hooking up with other people?" I asked casually.

She didn't turn to look at me as she said, "What do you mean?"

"Is it going to bother you if we hook up with other people?"

"We are friends, Mason." She finally looked at me. "Do you and Parker care if one of you hooks up with someone else?"

"No." I watched her eyes for any trace of something more

before I leaned in and whispered, "But I also didn't fuck Parker until he was screaming my name."

She blushed, just a trace of pink tinted her cheeks. "I wouldn't say that I screamed," she whispered back so Nate and Drew wouldn't hear.

"Yeah." I chuckled. "I guess it was pretty hard with Brandon in the next room."

She rolled her eyes, but there was a small smile on her lips.

"So, rule number two is neither one of us can get jealous?" I watched her.

"Agreed. No jealousy. Whatsoever."

"And if one of us does get jealous, we tell the other."

She nodded her head. "It won't happen, but agreed."

I followed her eyes to where she was now watching Drew and Nate who had left us alone at the table and picked up pool sticks.

"You want to play?"

"Sure. Against each other or you and me against them?"

"That depends. How good are you?"

"Good." I chuckled.

"Me too." She grinned. "Let's smoke their asses."

CHAPTER 11

DISTANCE

STACI

I COULDN'T STOP WATCHING the look on Nate and Drew's faces as they watched me sink shot after shot.

"What did you do, bring a pool shark with you?" Nate looked up at Mason who was watching me with a smirk on his face.

He shrugged his shoulders casually. "I told you she was awesome."

And just like that, I got those stupid damn butterflies in my stomach again.

I wasn't the kind of girl who got butterflies. I wasn't.

"It's not my fault you two kind of suck." I shrugged my shoulders at Nate and Drew, and Mason's smile widened.

"They do. Don't they?" Mason jabbed at them and both guys rolled their eyes.

I leaned down to take my next shot, a shot that would leave Nate and Drew with basically no chance at coming back. I squared up my pool stick, and I looked down the line to make sure it was my best shot. I took a deep breath to steady my hands and suddenly all of my breath was ripped out of my lungs as I felt a hint of a touch of callused fingers against the back of my thighs.

I closed my eyes momentarily and opened them to see Mason staring at me from where he now stood beside me. Friends my ass. Mason was still playing a game. A game I wasn't sure I didn't want to play.

I took the shot and missed.

Fucking missed for the first time that night.

My gaze jerked up to his and I bit down on the inside of my lip when I looked at that lethal smirk on his face.

"You got too cocky, Staci. It happens to the best of us." Nate moved around the pool table to line up his own shot, and I just smiled at him.

But Mason said nothing.

Not when I leaned against the wall next to him.

Not when I cocked an eyebrow at him waiting for whatever words I assumed he would spit out at me.

Instead, he just stared at my mouth. Stared at it like he was going to devour it at any minute, and I knew that I wouldn't stop him. I had no chance in stopping him.

His breath rushed out and I could taste the hint of beer and lust on my lips.

"Mason, you're up, man."

I blinked. Letting reality set in as Mason turned away from me and headed toward the table.

This was not supposed to be happening.

We were supposed to be friends. That was the only way this relationship, I cringed at the word in my own head, could work. Otherwise, one of us was going to get hurt. Because that's what Mason and I did. We hurt people. Not intentionally. At least that's what I told myself, but I refused to allow a man to get close enough to me to hurt me, and over the years, pushing guys away had somehow resulted in me hurting too many good ones.

But here I was watching Mason bend down and take the shot. I watched the way his back bunched under his t-shirt as he guided the pool stick between his fingers. I stared at his ass that looked ungodly perfect in his jeans, and I ran my fingers through my hair.

Mason Connor was not the guy I should be losing my head around. He was the opposite actually because for the first time in a very long time, I think I was truly at risk for a guy hurting me.

Just the thought had me setting down my own pool stick and heading to the bar. I could feel his eyes on me as I walked away, but I didn't care. Fuck, that was a lie. I was already caring too much, and that was why I needed another shot of tequila.

The bartender came up to me the moment I stepped up to the crowded bar and I ordered my shot. I turned my back to the bar as I waited for him to pour my choice of poison, and I looked around the bar. There were so many hot guys in that bar, but even glancing at them felt wrong somehow.

And it was exactly what I didn't want.

We were friends for fuck's sake.

I turned to face the bar again, and my gaze halted when it hit him. He was sitting on a bar stool, a beer in his hand, and he was watching me with a soft smile on his face.

Not the same predatory smile that he had been looking at me with earlier, but a smile that looked like he was happy. Happy that I was here. Happy that we were friends, and that smile was far more dangerous.

And even though it killed me to even think it, I knew that I needed to do something to distance myself from him because I wasn't going to get played by Mason Connor. I refused to get hurt, but something deep inside of me told me that I refused to hurt him as well. It was how I knew that this wasn't going to work. It wasn't going to go any further than this night.

CHAPTER 12

TEAMWORK

MASON

I WIPED the sweat from my brow as I stared around the house. We were finally down to the finishing touches.

It was one of the largest projects my company had ever taken on, and if I was being honest, it had scared me shitless when the client had decided to go with my company, a company that had far less experience than the competition, but they fell in love with my plan.

And I couldn't fuck this up.

There was too much riding on this project. Too much opportunity that would come from it.

"Knock knock." I heard my sister's voice before I could see her.

"In here," I yelled out as I watched her step over tools on her way to me.

"Do I need a hard hat?"

"Considering the walls are up"—I looked around the room at the finished walls—"I would say no."

She cocked her hip and rested her hand there. "Damn. I would have looked really cute in one."

I rolled my eyes at her then pulled her into a hug. She cringed at my sweat, but I didn't allow her to pull away from me.

"What do you think?"

She looked around the room as she wiped off her arm, and I tried to see it through her eyes. I tried to take it in as if I hadn't spent hundreds of hours working on it.

"Seriously, Mason." She turned to me. "It's phenomenal."

My chest bloomed with pride. "Thank you."

"Well, let's go. Give me a tour."

I took her around, room by room, showing her what we had done. Pointing out all of my favorite details.

When we got to the master bathroom, she sat down on the toilet and looked around. "No offense, but I kind of can't believe you did all this."

I huffed as I crossed my arms, and she held her hands up defensively.

"It's not that you did it. It's just that I can't believe I know someone who is capable of doing all this."

"Thank you for your backhanded compliment, Livy."

"You're welcome." She grinned then she narrowed her eyes at me. "Since we're in here all alone, I think it's time we had a talk."

"A talk about what?" I knew exactly what she wanted to talk about. My sister was sweet and sassy as hell, and if there was one thing I could count on her for, it was that she would always be nosy when it came to me.

"Staci."

"Ah." I rubbed the back of my neck, and I could feel the stress that had been building there. Stress that hadn't been there until the other night at the bar. The night that Staci went rigid as if I had done something wrong. Something that I had absolutely no idea what I did. One minute she was fine. The next, I could see it in her eyes. Her urge to run. To get away from me.

"What are your intentions with my best friend?" She crossed her arms and attempted to look intimidating.

"Shouldn't you be asking her what her intentions with your brother are? Plus, I didn't put you through this when we were in the opposite position."

"I have talked to her about her intentions, but you're the one I'm worried about. I'm not sure you have the best motives." She stood and made her way over to me.

"What did Staci say her intentions were?" I tried to ask the question casually, but I knew it sounded anything but. Because I couldn't figure the girl out if my life depended on it.

Livy narrowed her eyes farther. "She tells me that you two made a deal to be 'friends'." She actually did air quotes with her fingers when she said the word friends.

"We did." I nodded. "We're friends."

"I call bullshit."

I grinned at my ballbuster sister. "Why can't Staci and I be friends?"

"You have seen her, right?" She waved her hand in the air. "Staci is a freaking babe. There is no way you can just be her friend and not want to get in her pants." She stared back at me as she ran her fingers over the counter. "Again."

"I didn't say I didn't want to get in her pants. I just said that we were friends."

She watched me, and I could feel her assessing my every word.

"I'll ask you again. What are your intentions with my best friend?"

"Honestly?" I scratched at my beard that I hadn't shaved in several days.

Her face softened a bit, and she nodded her head.

"I'm trying to be her friend while simultaneously trying to not be friend-zoned. I'm trying my damnedest not to freak her out while she figures out that she wants to be more than my friend." It was the first time I had said those words, even to myself. It may have been the first time I really realized what the hell I was actually doing.

And it knocked the damn wind out of me.

I didn't do relationships. I didn't, but I was willing to try. For her.

"I knew it." She smiled, a huge smile, and I couldn't stop my own smile from taking over my face.

"You're not going to tell her, are you?"

"Are you kidding me?" She drummed her fingers together like she was some sort of evil witch. "I'm going to be the best wing woman you've ever had."

She put her hand out toward me waiting for me to put my hand over hers. "Go team Maci on one?"

"Maci?" I looked at my lunatic sister.

"Yeah. You know. Mason and Staci. Or we could do Stason, but that's a little weird."

"You're a little weird." I pointed out the obvious.

"Yes, but aren't you glad I'm on your team. Your love team." She made a heart with her hands and moved it back in forth from her chest.

I just walked away while shaking my head. She was right though, having her on my team was like having a trick play that Staci wouldn't see coming.

CHAPTER 13

CHICK FLICK

STACI

I GRABBED my phone out of my back pocket as I started cleaning up my station. I had just spent the last three hours working on a back piece and my hands were tired as hell.

"Hey, Dad." I plopped down in my chair.

"Hi, doll. How's it going?" His familiar gruff voice hit my ears, and I instantly smiled.

"Good. Just busy with work. You?"

"Everything is good." He cleared his throat, and I knew something was coming. "Ben came by here yesterday."

My lungs seized up at hearing his name coming from my father's lips.

Why the fuck would he go to my father's house?

Why couldn't he leave me alone?

"What did he want?" My voice sounded weaker than it did only a moment ago and that fact alone made me hate Ben even more.

"He said that he wanted to stop by and see you, but he knew good and well that you weren't here. He just thought he could pull a fast one over your old man. When I told him you weren't here, he asked for your number."

"Did you give it to him?"

"Hell no. I didn't give it to him." My father sounded good and angry. "I'm not sure what all went down between the two of you, but I'm smart enough to know that if that boy caused you to move several states away from me, then he did something to majorly fuck it up."

That was a complete understatement.

But my father was right. He didn't know what had happened between me and Ben. He didn't know the pain that he had caused me. I never told him. I still couldn't. Because as bad as Ben hurt me, I didn't want my father to hurt at the same time.

And he would.

That was the kind of man my father was. Anything that happened to me he put the blame on himself. Always.

When I didn't make the high school softball team, he said it was because he didn't help me practice enough.

When I broke my arm doing a trick on my bike, he said it was because he wasn't watching me.

When I had my heart broken by Ben, the first thing my father said to me was that it was his fault I didn't have a mother figure in my life.

And the look on his face destroyed me.

My mother left us when I was at the ripe old age of four years old, and she never looked back. I didn't know much about her besides the fact that I could be her twin. A fact I only knew from her pictures my father kept locked up in a box. Oh, and she was a worthless mother.

But my dad took the blame for that too.

He always had.

"Good. I don't want to talk to him."

It had been over three years since I had spoken to him. Three years since I had looked at his face. Just knowing that he was at my father's house, my childhood home, made my skin crawl.

"He wasn't too happy that I wouldn't give him your number, but you and I both know that boy doesn't have the balls to stand up to me. He just kept asking different questions, the same ones he asks every time I see him."

I knew the questions he asked.

He wanted to know how to get ahold of me. He wanted to know where I was.

But I had been out of his grasp for this long. There was no chance in hell I would allow him to find me now.

"Just avoid him." I picked at the tear in my jeans.

"I always do, but you're going to have to deal with him eventually. You can't do this forever."

"I know, Dad."

He huffed, a long, worried sound, and I squeezed my eyes shut.

"When are you going to come visit me anyways? It's been about six months since I've seen you."

"Hopefully soon," I lied. I didn't want to be anywhere near there if Ben was sniffing around. I needed to give him time to settle down and set his sights on something else. "I'll see when I can get off work."

"Okay, doll." I could hear the creak of his old chair that should have been replaced fifteen years ago. "I'm going to jump off here and get some work done around the house."

"It sounds like you're about to take a nap in your recliner," I teased.

His hearty laugh filled my ears and my chest ached with how badly I missed him.

"I never could get anything past you."

"Don't think you're going to start now."

I could practically hear his eyes rolling. "All right, girl. I love you."

"I love you too." I saw movement at the door to my station and looked up just as Mason walked in. "I'll call you later, okay."

"Okay."

"Bye, Dad."

Mason sat down on my stool across from me.

"Bye."

I clicked off my phone and set it down in my lap. Mason looked tired. He still looked hot as hell, but he definitely looked exhausted.

"Hey, Mason."

I twisted my neck from side to side trying to rid myself of thoughts of Ben. If I didn't get him out of my mind, it would fester, just like him, and I couldn't afford a sleepless night while worrying about him.

I was already missing too much sleep thinking about Mason and how I had left things the other night.

"Hey. You okay?"

His eyes were assessing me, and I knew that he was seeing too much. Mason always seemed to see past my bullshit.

"Yeah. Just tired." I climbed out of my chair and started finishing the cleanup I was working on earlier.

"You up for dinner?" He crossed his arms over his chest, and I watched how it made his muscles stand out more than they normally did.

"I don't know." I threw away the used ink. "I was thinking about going home and vegging out in front of the TV."

He nodded his head. "We can do that." His eyes lingered on my tattoo chair.

I shook my head at him. "I meant alone. You know, me, a big old t-shirt, a tub of ice cream, and a good chick flick."

He grinned at me, a devastatingly handsome grin, before shrugging his shoulders. "If we can throw in tacos before the ice cream, I'm down."

"You want to watch a chick flick with me?" I put my hands on my hips.

There was no way Mason wanted to come to my house to watch chick flicks. There was no way that I should let him.

"I would prefer to watch something with a little more action, but if it's what you need tonight, then that's what we'll watch."

I stared at him trying to see more of him than he was letting me. I didn't know what he was doing, what he was doing to me, but I did know that everything about him was fucking with my head.

I had made my decision the other night that I was going to push him away, a firm decision, but apparently it was deciding to be weak as hell in that moment.

"We're not cuddling." Because we were just friends.

"Of course not." He acted as if I had just offended him. "I don't cuddle during chick flicks. I need room to get all the feels."

A grin tugged on my lips. "Okay, Mr. Sensitive." I grabbed my purse. "Lead the way."

...

I had cried all the way through The Notebook, and Mason looked at me like I might be losing it. Hell, I might have been.

The tacos had been long since devoured, and I was moving on to the ice cream.

"Maybe we should watch something that is a little happier, next?" Mason was squatted down looking through my movies, and I smiled as he went through romance after romance.

"I'm a little surprised by your movie collection." He turned and looked at me over his shoulder.

"Didn't expect so many romances?" I pulled my spoon through the ice cream and plopped it into my mouth.

"Not really." He shook his head. "I'm just surprised is all."

My body tensed thinking about all the things he didn't know about me, about the things I didn't know about him, but I refused to think about that.

"Well, what did you pick."

He stood up from the DVD player and made his way over to the couch. The opening credits began, and he sat down right next to me. Far closer than he had been earlier.

"I thought I said no cuddling." I pointed my spoon to the seat he had sat in earlier.

"This isn't cuddling." He picked up the movie case that he had just set down on the table and held it up to me.

He had to be kidding me.

There was no way in hell.

Amityville Horror.

"This movie is scary." He fake shuddered. "If I sit way over there and you sit way over here, there is a bigger chance that one of us will be taken."

I rolled my eyes, but realistically there was no way in hell I would be able to watch that movie if he was all the way across the couch. I wouldn't let him know it, but the only reason I even owned the movie was because of Ryan Reynolds' abs. I didn't like scary movies. At all.

"You don't get taken because you're watching a scary movie."

He looked behind his back then looked back at me. "No, but it feels like you might," he whispered.

I laughed before I pushed at his shoulder.

"Fine." I waved my spoon at him. "You can stay where you are just so I can protect you."

"Thank God." He grinned right before he hit play.

CHAPTER 14

SLEEPOVER

MASON

SHE WAS SCARED SHITLESS.

I glanced over at her as she gripped the blanket in her hands so hard that her knuckles were turning white.

Her eyes were glued to the TV and if she didn't look so damn cute in her fear, I might have laughed. Instead, I touched my hand against her thigh. My plan was to comfort her. To let her know that nothing would touch her while I was here, but all I managed to do was scare her more.

She screamed, a sound that hurt my ears and probably woke her neighbors, and she swung out her arm and hit me dead in the chest.

"What the hell was that for?" I rubbed my chest where it was now aching.

"Are you insane? You don't touch someone in the middle of a scary ass movie. You're lucky I didn't kill you." She slyly looked behind her into the dark apartment, but I saw it.

"I was just trying to comfort you." I chuckled. "Plus, I don't think you could actually kill me."

"Don't underestimate me. My fight or flight skills are insane."

Screaming on the movie jerked her attention back to the screen, and she pulled the blanket higher over her body.

I watched her as she watched the rest of the movie. I didn't give a damn what was happening on the TV screen.

She flashed her eyes to mine as the credits began rolling, and I needed air. Being around her, becoming wrapped in her, I needed to clear my head.

"I'm going to head out." I stretched my arms above my head.

"What?" Her green eyes flicked around the apartment, and I had to hide my smile.

"I'm going to head home. I have to be on the job site first thing in the morning to meet the inspector."

I stood from her couch and grabbed our dinner trash from the table before carrying it to the kitchen.

"I could get that you know."

I gave her a look that told her not to mess with me, and she rolled her eyes before cuddling deeper into the couch.

"What time do you have to be at work?" She picked at the polish of her fingernail.

"I need to be there around seven. Why?" I threw our containers in her trash before shutting the lid.

"I just thought since it's so late maybe you would want to stay the night."

She avoided looking at me, and I couldn't hide my smile.

"I'll be damned." I chuckled.

"What?" Her eyes jerked up to mine.

"Never in my life would I think badass, Staci Johnson, would be so scared from a movie that she would need me to stay."

"I'm not scared." She threw her blanket down on the couch

before making her way into the kitchen where I stood. "I was just being nice since it's so late."

I grinned. "So, you'll be fine if I leave?"

"Of course, I will be fine, Mason. I do live on my own you know."

"Then I'll head home."

I saw the momentary panic in her face before she quickly hid it. "Fine."

She was leaning against the counter with her arms crossed, and I wanted nothing more than to kiss the stubborn look off her face. Instead, I put my hands on the counter at her sides and leaned into her space.

"Just say that you want me to stay, and I'll stay."

Her lips were just a whisper away from mine, and I could feel the heat of her breath.

"I was just being nice." Her eyes sparked with defiance, challenge.

"Okay. Then goodnight."

I leaned into her and brushed my lips against her cheek. Her eyes closed and her breath hitched so slightly that I barely even noticed.

But God, I noticed.

I pushed off the counter, leaving her standing there, but as I turned away, her small hand grabbed mine.

She took a deep breath and it was easy to see she was struggling with her decision, with her stubbornness.

"I want you to stay."

I could barely hear her words.

"What was that?" I cupped my hand around my ear and leaned toward her.

She rolled her eyes, which seemed like a constant when I was around, and said it again. "I want you to stay. Okay, ass?"

"All you had to do was say so."

She rolled her eyes again before she huffed, and I laughed as she walked away from me and headed into her room.

And I followed her.

She started throwing pillows off the bed before she started pulling down the blanket, and I took the time to look around her room.

There was floor to ceiling bookshelves covering one wall and every inch of space filled with books.

"I knew you liked to read, but I didn't realize you liked to read this much." I ran my finger across the spines as I took in the titles of the books. She had every type of romance novel imaginable.

"Yeah. It's my thing." She climbed into the bed and pulled the comforter up to her chin.

"You have a lot of things." I unzipped my jeans before pulling them down my legs.

"I'm not sure if that's a compliment or not."

"Well then I'm not going to tell you," I smirked before pulling my shirt off.

"Why are you taking your shirt off?"

"To sleep?" I held my shirt in my hand.

"You're at a sleepover. You don't sleep naked at a sleepover."

"You don't?"

"Have you ever been to a sleepover?"

"Yes. Me and my buddies have sleepovers all the time where we braid each other's hair and gossip about girls." I dropped my shirt on top of my jeans and climbed into her bed. She was lying on her side facing me, and my hand ached to reach out and push her black hair out of her face.

"I bet you and Parker did that shit all the time." She grinned.

"He tried, but he's really in touch with his feminine side."

She laughed as she turned away from me and turned off the lamp.

We were silent for several minutes with only the sound of our breathing filling the room.

"Are we going to cuddle?" My whisper broke the silence.

"No." She laughed. "You don't cuddle at sleepovers."

"Well shit. Me and Parker were completely doing this sleepover thing wrong."

She laughed as she buried her face in her pillow, but she didn't reach out for me.

But when I woke up the next morning, her body was wrapped around mine and I reveled in the feeling before she could wake up and pull away.

CHAPTER 15

FINN

STACI

IT HAD BEEN three days since Mason stayed over at my apartment. Three days that we had spent every day together. I was getting so used to him being in my space, and that scared the crap out of me. But he hadn't made a single move.

Not one.

We ate dinner. We watched movies. We laughed. Then he went home.

Every single night.

He never asked to stay. He hadn't touched me in any way that could possibly be misconstrued as inappropriate, and even though I had told him that was what I wanted, told myself that was what I wanted, it was driving me crazy.

My phone beeped on the table, and I smiled as I saw his name on my screen.

Mason: I had to go grocery shopping for you. You should feel special.

Me: I do. I know how hard that must have been for you.

Mason: It was. At least 3 different MILFs tried to take me home with them.

Me: You poor thing.

Mason: I know. They should have just put a price tag on me and put me in the meat department.

"What's that smile about? Who are you talking to?"

I looked up at Livy before tucking my phone in my back pocket.

"It's nothing. It was just Mason."

She grinned, and I pointed my finger at her. "No way. Get that little smirk off your face. Me and Mason are just friends."

She put her hand on her chest. "I didn't say you weren't. Don't get so touchy." She took a bite of her lunch. "What are you all doing tonight?"

"What makes you think we're doing anything?" I took a bite of my own burger and looked around the restaurant.

"Well, considering I've texted you every night this week to do something and you've been with him, I just figured."

"He's cooking dinner for me tonight." I popped a fry in my mouth as she almost choked on hers. "Are you okay?"

"My brother"—she pointed to her chest—"is cooking dinner for you?"

"Yes," I said cautiously.

She just nodded her head.

"What's that bullshit. Tell me what you were just thinking."

"I wasn't thinking anything." She swirled another fry in her ketchup and avoided looking up at me.

"Livy, I am your best friend. I know when you are lying to me."

She looked up at me then and studied me. "You're not interested in hearing what I have to say."

I rolled my eyes. "How could you possibly know that?"

"Because I'm also your best friend, and I know you."

"So, what? I'm not supposed to eat dinner with him. Friends can't do that?" I felt so frustrated, but I knew it wasn't her fault that she was just being honest with me.

"No. I'm not saying that."

"Then what are you saying, Livy?" I pushed my hair out of my face and looked at her.

"I'm just saying that I really like this whole you and Mason thing." She shrugged her shoulders.

"Me and Mason as friends." I reiterated the point.

"Yes." She rolled her eyes. "But you seem to have to keep saying those words out loud a lot."

"Trust me. I don't. He's made the point very clear." I regretted the words as soon as they slipped past my lips.

"What do you mean?" She leaned closer to me.

"I don't know. I think I just need to get laid."

"By Mason?" She looked confused. Confused as I felt.

"No. Not by Mason. Hell, I don't know what I'm saying."

"Are you sure that you just want to be friends with him?" She asked the question without a trace of judgment, and it was one of the things I absolutely loved about her. It didn't matter that it was her brother. Nothing mattered except the fact that I was her best friend.

"I just don't really know how to do the whole friend thing."

"That's not true. You're friends with Brandon and Parker."

"Yes, but I'm not attracted to either of them." I shuddered just at the thought. "They are more like brothers to me."

"Plus, you've never slept with them."

"That too." I put my face in my hands.

"Just think about your friendship with Mason like you would with me."

"That's impossible." I looked her over.

"How so?" She cocked her eyebrow at me.

"Because you don't make my lady parts tingle when I look at you."

"Eww, Staci." She leaned back in her chair. "We are still talking about my brother you know."

"Trust me, I know. But dear God." I closed my eyes and she fake gagged.

"It doesn't sound like you just want to be friends with him."

"It's not me." I batted my eyes at her. "It's my vagina. That girl can't differentiate the difference between our good friend Mason and the Mason who rocked her world."

"Then I guess you will have to be strong for the both of you." She smirked.

"Lord help us all."

Her laughter filled the restaurant as we finished our lunch.

...

I got out of my car and straightened my shirt. There was something about going to Mason's house for the first time that made my stomach flutter. It didn't matter that he had been to my apartment. I had the advantage there. I made the rules. But not here. Here I was in his domain.

My knuckles had barely touched the door before it was pulled open, and it left me with no time to school my features before my jaw hit the ground.

"You made it."

I barely even heard his words. I just stared at him. Every freaking inch of him that was on display.

He wiped his hands on a towel, and I watched as what

looked like powdered sugar or flour flew off his hands and landed on his very exposed abs. Abs that led down to that deep V of muscles that trailed beneath sweatpants that were slung low on his hips.

"Are you going to come in or are you going to stand on the porch staring at me?"

My gaze ran back up his body, very slowly, before finally meeting his. "Why don't you have a shirt on?"

He opened the door wider, and I shook my head to clear it before finally taking a step over the threshold.

"I never wear a shirt at my house." He shrugged before leaning into me. The smell of his cologne mixed with the hint of tomato sauce surrounded him, and I had to bite my lip not to groan. "But you better stop looking at me like that because we have a visitor."

"A visitor?" But as soon as the question left my lips, a loud commotion from what I assumed was the kitchen echoed throughout the house.

"Shit," Mason swore before taking off in that direction.

I watched as he ran through his house, and I shut the door behind me. I didn't know what kind of visitor he could possibly have, but there was something about it that instantly didn't sit right with me. If he had another woman here, I couldn't do it. I knew that we were just friends, but there was still a line.

At least for me there was.

I took a deep breath and took a step in the direction Mason had just disappeared.

Was he still sleeping with other women? The question had bounced through my head over and over the last few days.

Not that they were truly other women since I wasn't, I don't know, anything to him really, but the thought of him hanging out with me all evening then leaving to go sleep with someone else made my chest ache.

But I couldn't ask him. Definitely not in front of another girl.

I stepped into his kitchen and was knocked back a step when something ran straight into my legs. Not something exactly but someone. I barely caught him before he hit the ground.

"Who are you?" He didn't even wait until I put him back on his feet before he asked the question.

"I'm Staci." I glanced up at Mason who was stirring something on the stove. "Who are you?"

"I'm Finn." He picked up the ball from between my feet that he must have been chasing. "I'm Mason's best friend."

"You are?"

"Yup." He bounced the ball against the ground, and it flew back up into the air. "Are you his girlfriend?"

I glanced at Mason again and noticed the small smile that graced his lips before he turned toward his sink.

"No. I'm just his friend."

Finn tossed the ball toward me, and I caught it before tossing it back.

"Do you want to be my girlfriend?" He grinned at me, an almost toothless grin, and I couldn't help but laugh.

I sat down on the floor, and he sat down across from me. We began rolling the ball back and forth while I contemplated his question.

"How old are you?"

"Five." He held up his hand with all five fingers proudly in the air.

"There's a bit of an age difference. I'm twenty-four." I tapped my chin. "Do you have any other girlfriends?"

His little cheeks turned pink as he looked up past the island toward Mason. "Yes."

I shook my head and clicked my tongue.

"But only one more." He quickly said while looking back at me.

"Are you taking your dating advice from Mason? I don't date little players." I bounced the ball toward him, and he scrunched up his nose.

"Don't take it so hard, Finn." Mason moved around the island and set a bowl down on the kitchen table. "She won't date me either."

He winked at me as Finn's mouth dropped open and those damn flutters in my stomach started up again.

"My momma says that Mason's handsome." He threw the ball again, and it almost went past me.

"She does. Does she?" I cocked an eyebrow up at Mason.

"His momma is my next-door neighbor, by the way." He pointed out the window to the house next door. "She got called into work tonight and had no one to watch him. I didn't think you would mind."

"I don't." I quickly shook my head.

Mason reached down and scooped Finn up in his arms which led to a fit of giggles that escaped the little boy. He nuzzled his beard against his neck and little arms and legs flew in every direction as Finn begged him to stop.

Mason finally sat him down in a chair at the table before he laid an inconspicuous kiss on top of his head then he turned to me. I was pretty sure he could actually see my ovaries throbbing.

"You ready to eat?"

"Yea." I nodded before taking his hand he had reached out to me. His warm, callused hand gripped mine as he pulled me to my feet and right up against him. He leaned in close to me, close enough that Finn couldn't hear him, and I cursed the chill bumps that broke out across my skin as he whispered words into my ear. "You look gorgeous tonight."

"Thank you." I looked over his shoulder to Finn who was hitting his fork against the table.

Mason pushed my hair over my shoulder as he walked past me to the stove. The warmth of his fingers sinking into my skin.

"What are we having for dinner?" I took a seat at the table next to Finn, and he smiled up at me.

"Spaghetti. I hope that's okay with you. It's Finn's favorite."

"I love spaghetti too."

Finn held up his little hand to me, and we high-fived as Mason set a bowl of spaghetti on the table. He began filling our bowls with the pasta that actually looked delicious.

Finn reached his hand out for a piece of bread, almost knocking over his drink, and I noted little scratches on his elbow as he finally gripped the bread in his hand.

"What happened to your arm?" I reached for the bowl of spaghetti as Mason held it out.

Finn's face lit up. "I had a wreck." He lifted his elbow to try to see the small marks.

"What kind of wreck?"

"A bike wreck," Finn said through a mouth full of spaghetti. "I'm practicing for when I have a motorcycle like Mason one day."

My gaze jerked to Mason as he took a bite of his food.

"You have a motorcycle?"

He nodded his head and raised his eyebrows.

How the hell did I not know that?

"How the hell did I not know that?"

I stirred my own spaghetti and took a bite. The taste hit my tongue, and I groaned. It was so much better than I expected. It seemed Mason was full of surprises today.

"You never asked." Mason wiped spaghetti sauce off Finn's chin.

"That's not usually a prerequisite question I ask."

"For your friends?" He smirked.

"Yes. For my friends." I rolled my eyes. "I can't believe I didn't know you had a motorcycle."

"It's his only love."

"Shh." Mason laughed as he quickly put his hand over Finn's mouth.

"What?" He looked up at Mason like he was crazy.

"You're not supposed to tell all of my secrets, buddy. Some things are supposed to stay just between friends."

I grinned.

"But she said she was your friend." Finn looked over at me, confused.

"She is." Mason laughed. "But do you see how pretty she is."

They both looked up at me, and I tried to hide the fact that I was just shoving garlic bread into my mouth.

"Yeah." Finn nodded his head.

"When we have friends that pretty, we have to at least have some secrets from them." Mason winked at me, and I fought the urge to roll my eyes but couldn't hide my smile.

Finn studied me like he was trying to memorize every bit of advice that Mason gave him.

"Why do you have so many drawings on your skin?"

"I'm a tattoo artist. It's what I do. I draw on people's skin."

"Cool." He shot up in his chair. "Will you draw a tattoo on me?"

I looked to Mason, and he winked at me. A wink that did nothing to help me keep him in the friend-zone.

"After we eat, I will. Okay?"

"Okay." He sat back down on his bottom and started shoveling his food into his mouth.

Mason laughed and patted his little hand that laid on the table next to his.

"Now that I know you're so interested in my motorcycle, do you want to go for a ride tomorrow?"

"Seriously?" God, it had been so long since I had been on the back of a bike.

"Yeah. I don't have any plans tomorrow. Do you?"

I quickly shook my head no.

"We could go for a ride through the mountains. It's supposed to be nice tomorrow."

"For sure." Excitement filled me just at the thought.

"Then it's a date."

As soon as he said the word, another thrill went through me even though it wasn't supposed to. Even though I didn't want that from him.

"You can't date her. She's your friend."

We both looked down at Finn and his face now covered in spaghetti sauce.

"Thank you for reminding me. I almost forgot." Mason glanced up at me, and my stomach flipped.

"You're welcome." Finn tugged on my arm. "Can you draw my tattoo now?"

"Yeah." I could barely move my eyes away from Mason. "What do you want me to draw?"

"A dragon."

"Nothing simple then."

Mason chuckled, and I took the last bite of my food.

"Where do you want this dragon?"

Finn pointed to his right bicep and I nodded my head.

"Your mom won't get mad?" I glanced up at Mason.

"No. My mom is the coolest."

"She is." Mason backed him up.

"Okay. Then let's get my pens out of my car and I'll give you the most badass dragon tattoo ever."

Finn's eyes lit up then he turned to Mason. "She said ass."

CHAPTER 16

FRIEND ZONE

MASON

THEY HAD both been asleep on my couch for the past hour.

Finn's shirt was still off and his dragon tattoo that she had put an insane amount of detail into was on full display. He flipped his shit when he looked in the mirror after she finished.

He made me take pictures on my phone as he flexed his small muscles, and Staci giggled when he told me that his tattoo was way cooler than mine. She full on belly laughed actually, and Finn had helped me tickle her when she refused to tell me that he was wrong.

After the tattoo, we had watched a movie, a movie I had seen a million times with Finn, and the two of them had fallen asleep leaning against one another.

There was a small knock at my door, and I quietly lifted Finn from the couch before I carried him to the door where his mom was waiting.

"How was he?" she whispered before pushing his hair out of his face.

"Good as always." She went to grab him out of my arms and I moved out of her reach. "I'll carry him over."

She patted my arm and I could see the exhaustion in her eyes.

"Is that a dragon tattoo?" She touched his arm before pulling out her keys and leading the way over to her house.

"Yeah. My friend Staci drew it on him tonight. I hope you don't mind. He was so damn excited."

"Of course not. It will wash off." She waved her hand to dismiss my worry. "Is this the friend you were telling me about earlier?"

She stepped onto her porch before unlocking the door. I followed her inside, and Finn didn't shift an inch in my arms.

"Yeah. She came over for dinner tonight."

"Mason." She smacked my arm, barely making a sound. "You should have told me if you had a date tonight. I would have figured something else out."

"It wasn't a date. She only wants to be friends, remember?"

"Oh. I remember." She pulled down Finn's blanket, and I softly laid him down in his bed. "But I'm sure my son did nothing to help you get out of the friend-zone."

"What are you talking about?" I pulled the blanket up around Finn's shoulders. "Finn is the best wingman ever."

"Don't you be teaching him bad habits." She pointed her finger at me, and I chuckled as we walked out of his room.

"Never." I crossed my heart.

"Yeah. Yeah. Don't forget he's still at the age where he tells me everything."

She walked me to the door and leaned against it as I said, "He said ass tonight."

"Mason," she chuckled.

"Yes?" I batted my eyelashes innocently.

"Thank you for watching him."

"Anytime." I stepped off the porch.

"Oh, one more thing."

"Yeah." I turned back around to face her.

"Good luck getting out of the friend-zone."

"I don't need luck," I smirked. "I have a plan."

CHAPTER 17

BIKER FANTASIES

STACI

I WAS SO DAMN EXCITED about going on a ride with Mason that there was no chance in hell that I was going to be able to hide it.

Nothing else mattered today.

It didn't matter that I woke up in his bed, fully dressed under his blankets.

It didn't matter that he had breakfast cooked when I walked into the kitchen, and it didn't matter that I couldn't keep my eyes off of him while he held out a piece of bacon for me.

It definitely didn't affect me when he took that thumb that had just touched my lip and slipped it into his own mouth before sucking off the traces of bacon.

Nope. Definitely not.

He had grinned when I left his house to go get ready. He had instructed me to make sure I wore jeans and sensible shoes, and I rolled my eyes as I saluted him.

But God, I was excited.

The rumble of his motorcycle echoed through my apart-

ment, and I ran out to the parking lot with my small black backpack strapped across my back.

"It's not really fair." I pulled up to a stop next to him and
ran my fingers underneath my backpack straps.

"What isn't?" He had a pair of aviators covering his eyes,
and even though he looked insanely hot in them, I didn't like
that I couldn't see his eyes.

"How hot you look on a motorcycle."

"Oh yeah?" His smirk was so deep that I swore I could see a
dimple popping out under the beard he hadn't shaved in several
days.

"Yeah. Is it your ploy to pick up ladies?" I cocked my hip as
I slid my sunglasses over my eyes.

"Is it working?" He wagged his eyebrows, and I couldn't
help but laugh.

"Totally." I swung my leg over his bike and settled in
behind him. He curled his hand around the back of my knee
and jerked my body forward, pulling me closer to him. The
heat of his body radiated through my clothing, and I took a
deep breath to steady my thundering heart.

His motorcycle rumbled to a start, the rumble drowning out
every other sound, and I smiled as he hit the throttle and pulled
out onto the road.

My long braid whipped around me, the stray hairs sticking
to my face and neck, and I leaned my head back and let the
wind envelop me.

I had been on the back of a bike over a hundred times with
my father, and I missed this feeling. The wind. The freedom.

But this was different.

Being on the back of Mason's was different in so many
ways.

I felt safe with him, completely safe, but I also felt wild.
Like anything could happen at any moment. But I typically felt

that way with Mason regardless if I was on the back of his bike. There was just something about him that was unpredictable even though he was so sure.

I'd be lying if I said riding on the back of his bike didn't feed into every motorcycle club romance novel fantasy I had ever had. Because it did.

Every scene I had ever read was running through my head. The club, the motorcycle rides, the sex.

God, the sex.

But I was not supposed to be thinking about sex when it came to Mason.

Friends, friends, friends.

I chanted it in my head, but then the vibrations of the motorcycle and hardness of his body that fit perfectly between my legs cut through and all I could think about was sex, sex, sex.

I pressed my forehead against his back. He just needed to do something that would throw me off my game. Something that would seal him into the friend-zone. It really shouldn't be that hard. Parker and Brandon hit the friend-zone before I even thought about it. No effort.

Mason's hand settled on my thigh and his fingers pressed into me through my jeans, and all thoughts of friendship blew past me carried off by the rough wind.

We rode for over an hour, my body pressed against his for a full damn hour, and when we finally pulled to a stop outside an old bar-b-que restaurant, I could barely feel my legs.

Mason swung off the bike before gripping my hips in his hands and helping do the same.

"You been riding a lot before?" He unhooked my helmet and pulled it from my head. I was sure my hair was a wild ass mess, but at the moment, I didn't care. "You're a natural back there."

"Yeah." I took the helmet from his hands and strapped it to the back of his bike. "My dad had one practically my whole life."

He nodded his head and I could see a trace of relief in his eyes as if he knew I was going to say I used to ride with an ex.

I had been on the back of other bikes, but not with anyone who mattered.

"I hope you're hungry. This place has the best bar-b-que around."

"I'm starving." I followed him toward the restaurant, and he put his arm around my shoulders as we walked side-by-side.

We were sat as soon as we walked into the tiny restaurant, and I looked around at the red and white checkered tablecloths. The servers wore cowgirl boots and red plaid shirts, and I rolled my eyes when the server who came to our table accompanied her outfit with a pair of daisy dukes that were far too short to be serving food.

"Hi. I'm Brandi. I'm going to be your server today. Can I get you started with something to drink?" She had her eyes directly on Mason, not even acknowledging that I was there, and I could feel my claws coming out.

"I'll take sweet tea." Mason finally looked up at the server, but he only shot her a small glance before he turned to me.

"Sweet tea for me as well."

"I'll have them right out to you." Brandi stuck her pad of paper back into her apron that hung lower than her shorts and walked away after sparing another longing glance in Mason's direction.

I couldn't blame her.

He looked incredibly hot in a black t-shirt and jeans. His skin was tan, his aviators were resting on the top of his head, and his slight beard was begging me to grip it in my hands as I devoured his lips.

But I still didn't like her.

And I sure as hell didn't like her eye fucking my... my friend.

I unwrapped my silverware and put my napkin in my lap.

"What's wrong?" Mason smirked.

"Nothing's wrong." I pushed my hair out of my face and suddenly I felt self-conscious. I never felt self-conscious. Not over my looks. Not for a man.

It was something that I had promised myself a long time ago. I wouldn't change myself for a man, and I wouldn't let myself worry about it if he didn't love something about me.

But here I sat comparing myself to our server, and I fucking hated it.

"I'm going to run to the bathroom really quick." I stood from the table and headed toward the bathroom.

As I passed Mason, he touched his fingers to mine, bringing me to a stop, and he looked up at me with a big smile on his face.

"Have I told you today how beautiful you look?"

I took a deep breath and let it out slowly.

"Thanks, Mason." I let my fingers slip from his and pulled my braid over my shoulder, and just like that, the insecurities that were flooding me melted away.

I studied my reflection when I looked in the mirror then splashed water on my face.

I hadn't slept with anyone since that first night with Mason. I hadn't even thought about another man. I hadn't even realized it until that moment, realized the impact he was having on me, and I had absolutely no clue what I was doing.

But I knew for sure that I was getting in over my head.

I walked back to our table, and Mason smiled up at me as I sat down.

"Did you know that for every non-porn webpage, there are five porn pages?"

"Is that so?" I raised my eyebrows before taking a sip of my tea.

"Yup. It's a fact. I read it somewhere."

"Are you sure that you haven't been doing your own research?" I quirked an eyebrow.

"Do I look like the kind of guy who needs porn?" His grin was devilish and so damn handsome, and I knew that he wasn't. But I didn't want to think about that.

"So humble, Mr. Connor. Are there any other super-attractive characteristics I should learn about you?" I rolled my eyes, and he chuckled.

"Well, I wasn't going to tell you until it came out, but I also ordered your food for you."

My mouth fell open, and he held up his hands.

"You took so long in the bathroom, and I was wasting away to nothing out here. Plus, I think you'll be pleasantly surprised by what I chose."

"You think you know me well enough to pick my food?" I rested my chin in my hand.

"I think so." He nodded his head but looked unsure.

"How about a bet?"

His eyes flew to mine. "What kind of bet?"

"If it's not what I would have ordered off the menu, then you have to do whatever I say. If you get it right, I have to do what you say."

He stuck his hand out toward me. "Deal."

"We haven't even told each other the consequences of losing yet."

"So? Isn't life more fun that way?"

I went to slide my hand into his, but he pulled away.

"But you have to write your answer down on that napkin. I don't trust you not to cheat."

"Fine." I chuckled then he shook my hand.

When our food finally arrived at our table, I cringed at the bar-b-que pork quesadilla, and Mason's smile told me that he knew he had won without having to even read the napkin.

"Hand it over." He wiggled his fingers in front of me, reaching for the napkin.

"This is unfair." I tossed the napkin across the table before I picked up a piece of my quesadilla and took a bite. A delicious bite.

Mason just smiled as he unraveled the wad of napkin then he tucked it into his pocket.

"What? No gloating?" I took another bite of my food.

"Despite what you think, Staci. I'm actually a decent guy. I would never gloat."

"That just means my consequence is going to be bad."

His smile turned practically evil.

"What the hell are you going to make me do, Mason?"

"Patience, little one." He mocked me. "You'll see soon enough."

We finished eating our food with me mostly narrowing my eyes at him and him grinning like he had won the damn lottery. But it wasn't until Mason paid for our food and led me toward the very back of the restaurant that I became truly worried about what he was going to make me do.

"There is no way in hell." I slammed to a stop as soon as I saw it.

"Oh, yes. There is. You lost, sweetheart." He rubbed his hands together, and I looked around at all the people who were eating their food, yet looking up at us with interest.

I stared at the mechanical bull that looked three times my size before blowing out a deep breath.

"What kind of restaurant has a mechanical bull in the middle of the damn dining room?" I looked back at the way we came. If you didn't walk around the wall that was separating that part of the restaurant from this one, you would never know it was here. "How did you even know this was here?"

He shrugged his shoulders before leaning against the railing that blocked off the bull from the rest of the restaurant. "Servers are chatty when they think you're cute."

I rolled my eyes and turned back toward the bull. Out of all the crazy shit I had done in my life, I had never ridden a mechanical bull. Especially not in a restaurant that was full of strangers to watch me.

The bull moved an inch and I cringed. A hand slapped my ass as I took a step toward it, and I looked over my shoulder at Mason.

"Go get 'em, cowgirl." He winked at me, and even though I could kill him for making me do this, I also felt desperate to press my mouth against his.

I climbed up onto the bull which was an effort, and I gripped the handle in front of me before I looked at the guy who was about to throw me from the damn thing.

"You can only use one hand, cheater," Mason yelled across the restaurant, and I mean yelled. Anyone who wasn't watching me before turned their attention toward me.

But I did what he said and took one hand off the handle and flipped him the bird right before the bull started moving.

CHAPTER 18

RIDE EM' COWGIRL

MASON

I COULDN'T CONTROL my laughter as the mechanical bull bucked beneath her. She looked so damn determined up there. Determined to hang on or to kill me once she got off, I wasn't sure.

But fuck, she looked sexy as hell.

Her body rolled with each buck of the bull, her knees dug into its sides, and her hand was held up in the air. And my dick was instantly hard.

Hell, I was hard almost every second I was around her.

When she climbed on to the back of my bike, I almost groaned. When her body pressed up against mine, I had to close my eyes.

But I was willing to do whatever it took to get her to trust me. To trust me to be more than just her friend.

I wouldn't survive this friendship with Staci. I already knew it.

It would either go the way I wanted it to or I would get hurt.

But for the first time, I knew that the girl was worth getting hurt over.

I looked around and saw every other man's eyes on her, and instantly, I regretted my decision to make her ride that bull. They watched as her hips rolled back and forth. They stared as her chest shook with the force of the movement of the bull. I took a step toward the stand to tell the guy that it was time for it to be over, but then a smile broke across her face.

Not that damn fake smile that she so often used, but a real one, and it lit up her face.

She threw her head back and laughed as the bull started bucking harder. She started sliding to the left, but she was holding on for dear life. Her knees dug into the sides, and she gripped the handle harder.

The bull bucked several more times before she was finally slung off and onto the cushioned mat below. Her hair was covering her face and she just laid there in a fit of giggles.

After a few seconds, she finally stood and looked around at all the eyes that were watching her before she met mine. Then she leaned down and took a bow.

I joined the clapping and cheering that surrounded her, and when she jumped off the mat, I was right there to catch her.

"Today has been so much fun." She smiled up at me, and I knew, I fucking knew in that moment, that I would do whatever it took to keep putting that look on her face.

"The day isn't over yet." I grabbed her hand and pulled her back out to my motorcycle.

CHAPTER 19

SO MUCH FOR
A PRETTY DAY

STACI

I WATCHED the dark grey clouds hover over us as we continued our ride through the mountains, and I leaned in to talk in Mason's ear over the loud rumble of the motorcycle.

"Is it supposed to rain?"

Mason's gaze darted up to the sky before quickly returning to the road, and I huffed as he shrugged his shoulders. He had told me it was supposed to be a pretty day.

I looked back up to the sky just as a raindrop hit my cheek.

We were nowhere near home. Hell, I had no clue where we even were, but I knew it was going to be a long drive to get home.

Mason took a sharp curve to the left and more raindrops fell from the sky.

"Mason," I yelled at him, and the bike seemed to speed up just a touch.

There was basically nothing on the road we had been riding on for the last hour or so. I had seen a couple of gas stations and one restaurant along the way and that was it. I didn't know where he was planning on taking us, but I did know that our options were slim.

We rode for a few more minutes, the rain coming down in sheets now, my clothes completely soaked, before Mason finally pulled into an old gas station that looked like it had probably been abandoned over ten years ago.

The paint was chipped off the side of the building, the inside dark and absent of life, but there was still a roof that extended out over the long-forgotten gas pumps. We pulled under it before Mason killed the engine.

His foot kicked down the kickstand, and I pulled off my helmet before wiping the rain from my face.

"So much for a pretty day." I wrung out my braid and let the water drip down my body.

"A little rain never hurt anyone." Mason grinned before shaking out his hair.

Little drops of rain flew off of him, and his t-shirt clung to his chest and back. He lifted the shirt over his head to wring out the water, and I had to look away. I walked to the edge of the gas station and looked up and down the road that seemed to be reserved for only other motorcycles.

That was all that we had practically seen all day, but now there were none in sight. Probably hiding out from the rain like us.

I turned back to Mason, and he was leaning against the seat of his motorcycle watching me.

"How long do you think we'll need to wait it out?" I pulled my backpack from behind my back and grabbed my bottle of water.

"It's hard to tell." He looked up at the sky. "At least a little while I would say."

I held out my water to him, and he took it out of my hand before pressing it to his lips.

It was his lips. It was his eyes. Fuck, I didn't know what it was, but I couldn't stop. Once the thought ran through my mind, I couldn't fight it. Instead, I stepped in between his knees, and I stared at his damning mouth before I leaned into him and pressed my lips against his.

My water bottle hit the ground as Mason let it fall from his fingertips, but I barely even noticed the water that flew all over us. I was too busy focusing on the way Mason pressed his fingers into my hair, the way he gripped it roughly like he had been waiting for this moment for far too long. He tilted my head back, taking full control of the kiss, taking complete control of me.

He didn't give me a moment to regret my decision. Instead, he gripped my ass in his hands and lifted me in the air. He spun me back toward the bike and sat me down in the spot he had been in only moments before as he leaned into me.

His kiss was rushed and dangerous, far too careless to be anything other than pure need, and I ate up every second of it. When he pushed me further, I gave in. All fight had disappeared from me, and I had no intention of stopping.

His mouth moved over my jaw, dipping down my neck, devouring my skin. I reached out for his belt buckle, but he quickly pushed my hands away and kept kissing me.

He kissed me until I felt drunk just on the touch of his lips.

I looked down at his erection, reaching for him again, but his hand in my hair pulled back sharply. I groaned at the bite of pain and pleasure then ran through me when his teeth sank down into my shoulder.

Then he was gone.

I blinked my eyes open and whimpered when I saw him dropping to his knees in front of me.

His fingers quickly popped the button of my jeans, and I stood slightly as he shimmied them down my legs along with my panties. He made quick work of pulling them from my body.

It went through my mind at that moment that we were completely exposed, completely visible if anyone was to drive by, but that thought only lasted a second before I decided that I didn't care.

He pushed me back until my ass was once again sitting on his bike then his fingers slowly made their way up my legs. I was panting when his hands reached my inner thighs, and I wasn't expecting the way his fingers roughly pushed against the skin of my thighs. They fell completely open before him.

He looked up at me. He fucking watched me for every second of his descent toward my center, and I thought I was going to die by the time I felt his breath rush out against my skin.

"Whose pussy is this?" His words shocked me but had my body arching toward him involuntarily.

"Yours." I moaned and looked up at the roof that was still being pelted with rain.

"Look at me." His demand was firm, and I brought my eyes back to his. "Tell me."

I swallowed. I had never felt nervous during sex. I had never felt so high-strung, but with Mason everything was different.

"My pussy is yours," I whispered.

His answering smirk was dangerous and addictive, and I barely managed to take another breath before he jerked my right leg over his shoulder and dove into my flesh.

He wasn't in the mood to take his time or tease me. He devoured me. His tongue flicked against my clit piercing before he slowly sucked it into his mouth. I threw my head back, almost forgetting that I was sitting on top of his motorcycle, but he didn't seem to care.

He gripped my other leg in his hand and lifted it over his opposite shoulder before he pushed a finger inside me.

My fingers dug into the leather of his seat, my ass precariously on the edge, and I rode his face as he fucked me with his fingers.

It wasn't until I was screaming out his name that Mason finally stood from his knees. But he was far from done with me.

I stood on shaky legs as he turned me around until I faced the motorcycle, and a chill ran up my spine when I heard his zipper. His lips pressed against my neck and his hand kneaded my breast through my thin t-shirt.

"Mason," I breathed out his name.

"Put your hands on the bike, Staci. Don't move them unless I tell you to."

I trembled in his arms, but I did exactly as he had instructed. My ass was pressed firmly against him, and I swore as his hand ran over my ass before dipping between my legs. He gently teased my still pulsing clit with his fingers, and it was seconds before I felt like I was going to come again.

I felt him then, lining himself up with me, and he gripped my ass in his hands before he slowly pushed into me.

I bit my lip to stop myself from crying out as he pulled out of me then back in at an achingly slow pace. Over and over until I felt mad with lust.

I reached my hand behind me, trying to pull him closer to me, begging for more, for harder, but he was the one in control. He stilled inside of me as his hand came down against my ass, hard.

"What did I say, Staci?" he growled from behind me.

I whimpered and pushed back against him, my body begging him to move. He slapped my ass again, and my pussy tightened around him.

"You like that?" he whispered into my ear before his teeth sank into the sensitive skin.

"Yes," I moaned.

He nipped at my ear one last time before he leaned back away from me and gripped my hips firmly in his hands.

"Please, Mason," I begged him.

His control snapped then, and his bike felt like it was going to fall over from the force of his thrusts. My hands trembled against the seat as he slammed into me again and again. His hands bit into my skin, his need for me palpable in every touch.

I cried out when his fingers thrummed against my clit. My body shook, my orgasm consuming me. It stripped me of my ability to think straight. I wasn't thinking when my hand slipped. I wasn't thinking when Mason caught me in his arms without missing a beat, and I sure as hell wasn't thinking when the words I love you bounced through my mind.

My body tensed, everything went rigid, but Mason refused to allow me to pull away from him. Instead, he held me against him, his arms clinging to me as he thrust into me again and again, and when I finally cried out his name, I had never felt so scared in my life.

CHAPTER 20

THE MISTAKE

MASON

I HAD no damn clue what had happened.

One minute she was falling apart in my arms. The next I felt like she was a million miles away.

I had been wracking my brain trying to figure out what I had done wrong. Was it too much? Was it too soon?

None of it made sense. She had made the move.

I had no intention of pushing her further. Not yet. It wasn't part of my plan. I was still working on getting her to like me. I needed her to want to be with me before we were intimate again, but now everything was completely fucked up.

The entire ride home her body was stiff behind mine. Gone was the girl who felt carefree and happy behind me. The one who had leaned into me as she leaned her head back in the wind. The one who had wrapped her arms around me and squealed when I revved my engine.

She was gone.

Instead, I was left with the Staci that everyone else saw.

The one I was starting not to like.

I pulled up outside her apartment and took a deep breath as

I cut the engine. She didn't say a word as she slung a leg over my bike and got off without even giving me a chance to help her. She pulled her helmet from her head, her face completely hidden from my view, and when she finally turned back to me, that fake ass smile was back on her face.

But it wasn't until she pulled her phone from her pocket that I saw the girl I knew, the girl I was falling in love with, disappear.

"Thank you for the ride. I had a great time." She held my helmet out toward me, but I didn't grab it. Instead, I just stared at her. I stared at her and tried like hell to figure out what I could do. What I had done.

"What's wrong?" I finally asked as I pulled my own helmet from my head and ran my fingers through my hair.

"Nothing's wrong. Why would you think that?" Her hand was on her hip, and she had such a fake confidence about her. A look that said I didn't stand a chance against her, but I guess in reality I never did.

I motioned toward her with my hand, and I saw something flicker in her eyes. "Something is wrong. I know you."

"You don't know me." Her voice was low, and my body jerked back an inch at her words.

"I don't know you?" I questioned as I stood from my bike and she backed up an inch. "I think I know you pretty fucking well."

"You don't." She reached around me and set her helmet on the seat of my bike. "You only know what you want to know, Mason. But I'm not that girl. I'm fucked up." She stared into my eyes. "I'm not good at things like this." She motioned her hands between the two of us. "It's best we just end whatever the hell this is, now."

I let her words sink into me and panic like I had never felt before filled me. Panic to cling to her, to beg her to take back her words.

"I know that you eat ice cream like it's its own food group."

She rolled her eyes at my insignificant fact.

"I know that when you start to feel sad, you only listen to Ed Sheeran and you mouth the words to the songs even when you're tattooing. I know that you are a fiercely loyal friend, and my sister is damn lucky to have you."

I took a small step toward her and she turned her head to look away from me.

"I know that you snort just a tiny bit when you think something is really funny and you gasp for breath when you cry from a sappy chick flick. I know that you hide behind this hard, bad girl shield to keep people at a distance, but you have a wall full of romance books in your room and you look like you are falling in love again and again every time you're reading one."

"Mason." She twirled the end of her braid in her hand and looked up at her apartment.

"I know that you push me away because you're scared of what we could be. Of what we are becoming."

I watched her then. I watched her close her eyes and take a deep breath. I watched her brace herself for whatever she was going to say next, and I should have done the same. I should have protected myself from her. But I was an idiot.

I was an idiot who didn't even see it coming.

She turned her eyes back to me, and I hated what I saw there. I fucking hated it. "I'm not interested in anything more with you, Mason. I fuck. That's it. I don't date. I don't have relationships. I tried to make that clear to you in the beginning. This"—she motioned between the two of us—"this was a mistake. We had no business being friends, and we sure as hell had no business fucking again if you couldn't keep your feelings out of it."

I stepped back as if she had struck me.

"I'm sorry if—"

"You're not sorry," I cut her off. "You're a coward."

Her mouth straightened into a hard line, but her chest rose and fell as if she was having a hard time breathing.

"I didn't want to hurt you," she said the words softly, but I didn't believe any of it.

"Save it, Staci." I strapped my helmet on and moved back onto my motorcycle. Everything inside of me was telling me not to leave, but I wouldn't allow Staci Johnson to drain even one more ounce of my pride. "I get it," I said the words over the rumble of my bike. "You let me fall in love with you only to truly fuck me in the end."

Her hand reached out, only minutely as pain fill her face, but I wasn't going to stand around and watch it. I wasn't going to let her drag me back in to only kick me out again. So, I kicked up the kickstand, and I rode away from her. I didn't dare look back because I knew that I was too weak when it came to her. And this was exactly why I shouldn't let myself do this.

I broke my own rules, and I could only blame myself.

CHAPTER 21

GOING HOME

STACI

I COULDN'T BREATHE.

I couldn't fucking breathe.

I sank down to the floor as soon as I managed to close the door, and I buried my face in my hands. I was such a damn idiot.

Mason was right. I was a coward.

But God, I panicked.

I panicked and pushed him away before I could even let the thought run through me. It was what I did. I pushed people away. I usually never let them get close enough to hurt me, but I had fucked up with Mason.

I knew from day one that we would hurt each other, that I would hurt him, but I was a fool. For the first time in as long as I could remember, I had let my guard down around a guy, and it was a mistake.

Mason was too much. He was too powerful. Too potent.

I didn't stand a chance, and Mason deserved more than what I could give him.

My phone buzzed in my pocket, and I pulled it out to see

my dad's name light up on the screen. I took a deep breath, as deep as I could, and pressed answer.

"Hey, Dad."

"Staci, it isn't looking good, doll."

I winced and rubbed my face. "What did the lawyer say?"

"You're going to have to come back. She said that Ben is asking for mediation."

"I'm not doing mediation with him. Why can't she just go to court and be done with it?" I let my head slam back against the wall.

"Because if you don't agree to mediation, then he's going to try to take the house." My dad's voice was soft, wary.

"He can't take your house."

"He can. You and I both know it. It's in your name, Staci. He can go after anything he wants."

I gripped my hand against my thigh to keep myself from screaming. "I don't understand what he wants from me."

I didn't understand why he wouldn't just let me go.

"From what your lawyer told me, he wasn't very happy when he was served the divorce papers. I think the word she used was enraged, actually. She doesn't think he's going to do any part of this easily."

I didn't know why I ever thought he would. He had never done anything easily. He had never cared about anyone other than himself.

It was why I had left. He was why I had left the only home I had ever known.

"When do they need me there?" I asked, but my skin crawled just thinking about it.

"She said if you agree to mediation that she could get it scheduled as early as next week. She said that Ben is trying to push everything back, but he agreed to that."

Of course, he did.

Because he knew it would get me home. He knew that I would never allow him to take my father's home. A home he had worked his whole damn life for. A home he had put in my name in case anything had ever happened to him, and here I was, putting everything he worked for at risk.

"Okay. I'll talk to Parker today and see what I can figure out with work then I'll get a flight."

Dread. Pure fucking dread filled me.

"Call me and let me know the plan. You better tell me when your flight gets in so I can pick you up at the airport. I'll be damned if you take a taxi like last time."

"I will, Dad." I laughed softly.

Even though going home to deal with Ben was by far the last thing I wanted to do, I did miss my dad. I missed him far too much, and I was dying to see him. Dying to have him hold me in his arms and tell me that everything was going to be okay.

Because right now, everything I could see, everything I touched, it was all fucked up.

CHAPTER 22

TIME

MASON

IT HAD BEEN over a week since I last saw her. A week.

And I had regretted my decision to ride away from her for every damn second of it.

I had gone back to her apartment the next day. I was prepared to prove to her that she was wrong. I would force her to face the truth if I had to. Because I wouldn't just walk away like this. I wouldn't let us end like this.

But she was gone.

Her apartment was dark and the door locked, but her car was still in the parking lot. I had called her phone probably five times over, but it had gone straight to voicemail each time.

I felt like I was going crazy.

Parker probably thought I was crazy as well. I banged on his front door, banged on it repeatedly until one of them answered. He looked at me like I had lost my damn mind when I walked past him into his house, but I didn't care. I needed to talk to my sister. If anyone knew where she was, it was her.

She was in the kitchen when I walked in, but I didn't care

what she had going on. I only cared about one thing. I could only think about Staci.

"Where is she?" I grabbed her shoulder and turned her to face me.

"Who?" She looked up at me confused.

"Don't act dumb. Staci. Where is she?"

Livy jerked away from my touch and pushed me hard in the chest. "Don't you come into my house and call me dumb. I don't know what the hell you're talking about."

I ran my hands through my hair, frustrated. "I went to her apartment and everything is off, but her car is there. I tried calling her phone and it goes straight to voicemail. I need to see her. After yesterday—"

"What happened yesterday?" she interrupted me and put a hand on her hip.

I swallowed as I let the memories flood me. "I don't know." I threw my hands up in the air. "We went for a ride on my motorcycle yesterday morning, and everything was perfect. We were having a great day. She was happy, she was smiling, then poof." I snapped my fingers. "Everything changed."

"It couldn't change just like that. Something had to happen."

Parker walked up behind Livy and pulled the spatula from her hand that she was waving in the air before going to the stove.

"Well, we had sex." I shrugged my shoulders.

"Mason," she growled. "Did I tell you nothing? That was not a part of the plan. You were supposed to be wooing her not fucking her."

"You two had a plan?" Parker looked over his shoulder at us, but Livy ignored him.

"So, what? Was it bad?"

"No. It wasn't bad," I huffed. "It was amazing actually."

"At least for you," she said under her breath.

"It wasn't the sex," I growled. "But afterward it was like something just changed. Something happened. I just don't know what."

Livy picked up her phone and hit a few buttons before she pressed it to her ear. I held my breath as I waited to see if she would answer, but Livy made a perplexed face and set the phone back on the counter.

"Straight to voicemail."

"I told you."

Livy rolled her eyes and crossed her arms. "Why would she have her phone off? That doesn't make sense."

"She's on a plane."

We both turned and stared at Parker when we heard his words.

"What?" I asked as Livy said, "How do you know?"

Parker turned off the stove eye before he turned to look at us. "She called me last night to tell me that she needed to go home to take care of some things. She's going to be in Oklahoma for a few weeks."

"Why didn't she call me?" Livy looked offended.

"Well, she called me to make sure I could move things around for her at work. I'm sure she'll call you once she gets things settled down."

"What does she need to take care of?" I tried to think of why she would need to go home. She never talked about Oklahoma. She avoided talking about it actually.

"That's something that you will need to talk to her about." Parker was looking directly at me, and I knew that he hated keeping this from me. We didn't keep shit from each other. Never had.

Except for my sister.

"How am I supposed to ask her if she won't talk to me?"

"She's on a plane, Mason." My sister rolled her eyes.

"No." I shook my head. "She told me yesterday that she didn't want to do this anymore. She said a lot actually."

"Give her time." Parker pulled three plates out of the cabinet.

"Time." I nodded my head. "I'm sure that will be easy. What if giving her time just fucks everything up more?"

I looked from Parker to my sister and neither one of them said anything for a minute.

But then my sister smiled. "Then you can kick Parker's ass for suggesting it."

CHAPTER 23

THE PAST

STACI

THERE WAS nothing in the world that I could do that would help me be prepared for the meeting I was walking into. It had been three years since I had laid eyes on him. Three years since I ran away and never looked back.

My dad had offered to come with me, but I refused. I needed to do this on my own. I needed to face him regardless of how badly I didn't want to. Regardless of how badly he had hurt me.

He stood as my lawyer and I walked into the room, and I avoided looking in his eyes. He looked the same as he had the day I left. His light brown hair styled back out of his face and not a single hair out of place. It never had been. He was wearing a pair of khaki pants with a light blue button-up shirt. A light blue that I knew were bringing out the ocean blue of his eyes.

His cologne hit me as I reached the large table, and I closed my eyes and tried to force out all the memories that were flooding me. Memories that I hadn't thought about in a very long time. Memories that I refused to allow me to feel weak again.

"Mrs. Callen." Ben's lawyer nodded his head to my lawyer before turning to me. "Mrs. Howell, please have a seat."

My lawyer started to sit, but I didn't.

"My name is not Mrs. Howell." I stared at him. "I am Ms. Johnson."

"With all due respect, ma'am, you are still married to Mr. Howell, and as such, your name is still legally Mrs. Howell."

"With all due respect, sir." He reared back at the venom in my voice. "I am Ms. Johnson. My legal name has been changed to Ms. Johnson. If you would like me to stay for this mediation, you will refer to me as such."

Ben's soft chuckle was like fingernails down a chalkboard.

I finally looked at him, really looked at him, and I didn't know why I expected to see anything different. But the man staring back at me with a smirk on his face was the same exact monster I had left three years ago.

I pulled my gaze from his and took a seat at the table as far from him as I could. My lawyer's hand touched mine under the table, a silent sign of her support, before she began.

"You all have asked us here for mediation in agreement that you will no longer go after her father's home." His lawyer nodded his head in agreement. "So, please inform us what exactly you have asked us here for. Mr. Howell already has the home that they once shared along with their vehicles and all of their belongings. When Ms. Johnson left, she didn't take anything that belonged to him."

Ben scoffed, but I refused to look at him again.

"Mr. Howell would like to discuss the terms of the divorce. My client feels that he and Mrs."—he cleared his throat and corrected himself—"Ms. Johnson didn't give their marriage a fair chance. He would like Ms. Johnson to consider counseling before going forward with the divorce. Otherwise, he will refuse to sign the papers without going to court."

I clenched my hands into fists and counted to ten. "Can Mr. Howell and I have a moment alone?"

My lawyer looked at me with shocked eyes. "Are you sure that's a good idea?"

"I'm positive." I looked at Ben, and he was leaned back in his chair completely relaxed.

"I'll be right outside the door."

I nodded my head to her but didn't take my eyes off him.

When the door clicked shut behind me, he finally opened his mouth.

"It's nice to finally see you, love." He leaned forward, and I cringed that he was even an inch closer to me. "Although, I could have done without all the trashy tattoos but you can always cover those with clothing."

"You have lost your damn mind if you for one second think that I would be willing to even consider giving this another chance."

He tsked, something I absolutely hated about him, and smiled at me.

"You don't have too much of a choice. You can either agree to counseling or I will drag your ass through court. I know that your daddy's old house is in your name, and I know that you probably have assets wherever the hell you've been."

But he was wrong.

It was the reason I didn't own my own house. It was also the reason I turned Parker down when he offered to allow me to own a third of Forbidden Ink.

Because I knew that Ben would try to ruin everything.

But I refused to let him know that. I refused to let him know how much he affected every decision I made.

"You won't."

Ben laughed, a laugh that I fucking hated, and placed both of his hands on the table between us.

"You don't think I would do it? You don't think I would take your dad's house right out from under him? You don't think I would take everything away from you?"

"You've done it before."

He grinned. "And I will do it again."

I leaned down and pulled an envelope out of my purse. I hadn't looked at it in over two years, but I knew every detail of what laid inside.

Every inch of it was burned into my brain.

I pulled the pictures out one by one and laid them in front of him.

He didn't say a word as I set them down. He just stared at them with fury in his eyes, but he didn't know fury. He hadn't even begun to taste the amount of rage I felt toward him.

I pressed the last picture against the table then I folded my hands in front of me.

"If you even try to take me to court, I will bring every one of these with me." His eyes bounced up to mine. "These pictures." I pointed down at the images of my body covered in bruises. "These are only the last time. I have plenty other pictures where these came from." I didn't, but he didn't need to know that. This was the only time I had gone to the hospital. It was the only time I had gathered my courage and my hate and decided to leave.

"You can't prove that I did that." He looked up at me, and every ounce of hate that I had for him boiled up inside of me.

"I will blast this everywhere, Ben." His eyes narrowed at me. "How do you think the other men at your firm will feel about this? How will your parents feel about it?"

He didn't say a word. He just stared.

"I won't stop until I've ruined you. If you want to play this game with me, then we'll play it. I'm not the girl in these pictures anymore." I pushed one closer to him so he could see it, so he could be reminded of the pain he had caused. "If you refuse to sign those papers today, you will regret it."

"And if I do sign them?" His throat bobbed, and I knew that I had him by the balls.

"Then these pictures will go back to where I've had them all these years. You'll never see me again, and I will never hear from you again. You sure as hell will not go to my father's house looking for me. This will be over."

He swallowed hard, swallowing the words I was sure he was dying to spew at me, then nodded his head.

I looked behind me and waved our lawyers to come back in. When they did, Ben's lawyer stopped mid-stride as he looked at the images that still rested on the table.

"Mr. Howell?" His voice was low and questioning.

"We're both prepared to sign the divorce papers today." His gaze flew to me. "I'm happy that you both demanded we attend mediation. Aren't you, Ben?"

But that motherfucker refused to look at me again, and I decided that I no longer cared. Once I left this room, I was leaving all of this behind me. Him, the ghost that haunted me, and every ounce of pain that had held me hostage over the last three years.

CHAPTER 24

VEGAS

MASON

STACI WAS STILL GONE.

It had been three weeks since I had seen her.

One text. That was it. One measly little text message was all that I had gotten from her.

After I had called her three different times, the only response:

I'm sorry.

I was so damn angry I couldn't see straight. She was sorry? I didn't want her apologies. I wanted to know what the hell happened. I wanted to know what I had done.

"Calm down." My sister was typing on her computer and watching me like I was crazy as I stared into Staci's tattoo room. A room that hadn't been touched since she left. "You will see her in Vegas."

"She's coming?" My eyes darted to my sister.

"Of course, she's coming. Her, Parker, and Brandon are all three being featured at the convention, and it has been planned for over a year. She kind of has to be there."

"And I have to be there, why?" There was no way in hell I

wasn't going now that I knew she was going, but Livy was still adamant that I be there.

"Because I'm tired of watching you mope. Staci will be there, you'll be there. Maybe the two of you can finally make up or get your shit together or whatever you need to do."

"I haven't been moping." I leaned against the counter.

"Yes. You have." Brandon's voice carried from his room.

"Fuck you, Brandon."

He chuckled then started talking to the guy he was tattooing.

"We leave at seven in the morning, so I need you to make sure that you are completely packed tonight and are at the house by four thirty."

"You don't have to worry about me. I'm the responsible one. You need to talk to your boy Brandon."

"I can hear you, asshole."

I smiled at my sister.

"Don't worry. I'm making him stay the night with me."

I chuckled as we heard Brandon talking to his client again. "They are a pain in my ass."

...

I had no idea what we were doing. All I knew was that I was instructed to be in the hotel lobby by seven o'clock sharp by Livy and to wear something nice.

We had arrived in Vegas around noon, and the four of us came straight to the hotel where I took a nap. I didn't know if Staci was already here. I hadn't seen her, and no one had mentioned it either.

But I was dying to see her.

I knew there was no way that I wouldn't go looking for her, so when Parker and Livy told me they were going to check out the casino, I left them on the casino floor and Brandon already talking to some chick while I went up to my room.

Now I stood in the hotel lobby alone, and I can't stop searching every face in the crowd for hers.

I straightened my jacket and cringed at the black pants and jacket Livy told me to pack. I wasn't really a suit kind of guy, but Livy was adamant and impossible to say no to.

I looked up just as the elevator door opened and Staci stepped out. She was laughing at someone behind her, and I clenched my fist when I saw Brandon walk out behind her.

I had no right. Brandon was her friend. Hell, he was my friend, but it still made me insanely jealous to watch her with him.

It made me downright angry.

Staci's gaze hit mine and her steps faltered.

She didn't know that I was here. I could read it all over her face. She had no idea, and she hated it.

She hated that I was here, and she hated that she wasn't prepared.

I could see the wheels turning in her head, trying to think of what she was going to say to me.

I couldn't take my eyes off her. I hadn't seen her in weeks. I had been going crazy, but here she was in front of me, just as fucking beautiful as the last time I saw her. Somehow more.

I just stared at her as she walked toward me, but as soon as I saw the woman walking around the corner behind her, my heart completely stopped.

Staci noticed my gaze move away from her, and she coyly looked over her shoulder to see what had grabbed my attention.

But none of us were expecting what we saw.

My sister was walking hand in hand with Parker, and she was wearing a short white dress and carrying a bouquet of flowers in her hand.

"What the hell?" Brandon reached his arms out for my sister, and she ran into them with a squeal.

"We wanted to keep it a secret." Livy laughed as she looked over at Parker while a smile took over her face.

"You two are getting married?" Staci sounded as shocked as I felt.

"Yes. Man, that sounds crazy. We're getting married."

Staci grabbed my sister's hand and twirled her in a circle to look at her dress, and they both looked so damn happy. Parker reached his hand out to me and I shook it before I pulled him into a hug.

"I'm so happy for you, man."

"Yeah?" He chuckled as he clapped my back.

"Absolutely."

He pulled away from me and rubbed his hand over the back of his neck. "Does that mean we have your blessing?"

I looked my best friend in the eye. "Are you asking for my sister's hand in marriage?"

"I am." He looked so uncomfortable, and I wouldn't be the good best friend that I am if I didn't let him at least sweat it out a bit.

It wasn't until he narrowed his eyes at me that I said, "Of course, you have my blessing."

"Well, let's go get married." He smiled then and I knew that I would never again have to worry about my sister being happy.

CHAPTER 25

THE WEDDING

STACI

I HAD NEVER SEEN Livy or Parker so happy in all the time that I had known them.

When we got into the limo that pulled up outside of our hotel, Parker popped a bottle of champagne to celebrate before we ever made it to the chapel. We clinked our glasses and I laughed with my friend, but I couldn't avoid the fact that Mason had been staring at me since the moment I saw him in the hotel lobby.

I wished Livy would have told me he was coming so I could have prepared myself, but I knew why she didn't. I probably wouldn't have come, and I would have hated myself if I missed their wedding.

The Elvis impersonator greeted us as we walked in the door of the chapel, and Livy's laughter only fueled everyone else's.

"You're my maid of honor." She bumped into my shoulder like it was no big deal.

"Of course."

"And you two." She pointed at Mason and Brandon. "I

know that Parker told you that you are sharing the position of best man, but Mason, you have to walk me down the aisle first."

I could see the emotion in his eyes as she said the words. The two of them had been basically all each other had for so long.

Mason nodded his head and straightened his jacket.

Parker, Brandon, and I made our way through the chapel and took our places. Parker didn't look nervous at all. He looked grounded and blissfully happy.

It struck me then that we could have been at a wedding where he married Emily. He could have made the biggest mistake of his life.

A mistake like I had made when I was eighteen years old.

My wedding was nothing like this.

Between my dad and Ben's parents, they spent a small fortune on our wedding day. There were flowers everywhere. Flowers that I hated, but his mother said were classic and tasteful as opposed to the yellow daisies I wanted.

And my dress was the worst thing about it.

Because I looked like someone who was the opposite of myself. Someone I had pretended to be for years.

But Livy, God, she looked so gorgeous and so happy as she walked down the aisle on her brother's arm. She didn't wear a coy smile as the photographer that came with the chapel started snapping photos of her. No. Livy's smile took over her face as she leaned into her brother.

Mason took his place behind Parker after he placed Livy's hand into his, and everyone laughed when Livy whispered, "Holy shit. We're doing this."

Then Elvis started talking and the whole damn thing was magical.

"The bride and the groom have prepared their own vows," the Elvis impersonator said with his horrible Elvis voice.

Parker cleared his throat as he pulled a piece of paper out of his pocket that looked like it had been wadded up then straightened back out at least ten times.

He took a deep breath and looked up at his girl. "Livy, I don't really remember the day that I fell in love with you because I feel like I have been cliff diving into you since I was sixteen years old. I never stood a chance. You were always the only choice, and I do choose you. I choose you to be the one who I walk through this life with. I choose you to fight with. I choose you to make up with. I choose you to be the one who pushes me to be a better man, and I choose you to be the one who talks during movies even though you know it drives me crazy. I will choose you every day for the rest of our lives because I swear that I couldn't love you any more than I do now, but God, I know I will fall more in love with you tomorrow."

I wiped at my eyes as I watched tears stream down Livy's face. She pulled a piece of paper out of the pocket of her dress and shook out her trembling hands.

"No pressure, huh?"

Everyone laughed including Elvis then Livy took a deep breath.

"Even though I am unsure about most things in life, I know with everything inside of me that I love you and will love you forever. I know that we will face many trials together, but I vow that we won't face them alone. I vow to always laugh at your jokes even when they are questionable, and I vow to try my hardest not to use all of the hot water. I vow to pick you up any time you are down and to always remind you why we fell so madly in love with each other. More than anything, I vow to love you fiercely for the rest of our days. I love you."

"By the power vested in me by the State of Nevada, I now pronounce you husband and wife. You may now kiss the bride."

Parker reached out for Livy and dipped her back as he devoured her mouth with his. Mason and I cheered while Brandon catcalled, and Parker took his time kissing his wife before he straightened her back to her feet.

"Ladies and gentlemen"—Elvis shook his hips—"it is my honor to present to you Mr. and Mrs. Parker James."

Parker bent down and scooped Livy into his arms and carried her back down the aisle bridal style while she laughed uncontrollably, and I knew in that moment that I would never get married again. Not until I found a love like that.

CHAPTER 26

THE FREE FALL

MASON

MY SISTER and best friend were married.

They were married and so deeply in love, and for the first time in my entire life, I felt truly jealous of what they had.

We had been celebrating for the last hour or so, and Staci had managed to avoid me for the entirety of it. She had barely even looked my way.

But I was tired of it.

Livy and Parker were out on the dance floor, and Staci was taking a shot at the bar with Brandon. She had been drinking since we had arrived at the club. Far more than I had ever seen her drink before.

I walked up beside her at the bar and reached for the next shot she was about to take. She narrowed her eyes at me as I threw it down my throat, but she didn't say a word to me. She just held out her hand for the bartender and ordered another shot.

I could tell she was drunk, and I knew that it wasn't the time or place to have an argument with her, but I couldn't just stand back there watching her while she pretended like I didn't exist.

"I think you've had enough. Don't you?"

Brandon raised his eyebrows before he picked up his own drink off the bar and walked away.

"I'm pretty sure I already have a dad, Mason, but thank you for your concern." She patted my chest with her hand, and I felt that touch like a brand.

"Do you?" I cocked an eyebrow at her.

"I wouldn't know considering you never tell me anything."

She started to turn away from me, but I touched her cheek to stop her. "Like where the hell have you been for the last three weeks?"

"I went home to see my dad." She pulled her face away from my touch.

"Just like that. You decided to go and left without saying anything."

"I don't have to tell you what my plans are, Mason. I don't owe you any sort of explanation."

"Don't you?"

She looked away from me again, but I wasn't done with her.

"So, what? You get to tell me to fuck off and because you said so, I'm supposed to just stop having feelings for you?"

"You don't have feelings for me, Mason." She stepped away from me, but I followed her.

"You don't get to tell me what I feel."

She kept walking ahead of me, but I knew she could hear my words. I knew they were affecting her.

"Just stop, Mason." She spun toward me and I almost ran into her. "I'm done talking about this. I'm going to my room. Just let me go. Okay?"

"Okay." She looked as shocked by my words as I felt. "But

you're not walking to your room alone. I'll walk you there then I will leave you alone."

She rolled her eyes, but she didn't argue as she led the way to our rooms that were all beside each other.

We walked down the hallway to the elevator which was packed with people who were either leaving the club or the casino, and I couldn't help but smile when she was forced to stand right on top of me due to the lack of space.

Her arms were crossed and she refused to look at me as the elevator stopped floor by floor letting people off, and as soon as there was enough room, she moved away from me as if she was on fire.

An older gentleman at the other side of the elevator raised an eyebrow at me. "Lover's quarrel?"

Staci's gaze jumped up to him before she turned to look at me.

"Something like that."

Staci huffed, but the man just continued.

"My wife has always been stubborn as a mule too, but let me tell you, son, she's worth it."

I started to reply to him, but Staci beat me to it. "I am not stubborn, and I am not his lover." She hiked her thumb over her shoulder to point at me.

"Could have fooled me, sweetheart." He winked at her as the elevator came to a stop, and he walked off.

"The nerve of some people," Staci mumbled to herself but still didn't look at me.

When the elevator finally stopped on our floor, she was walking out the door before it had completely opened.

I could feel the anger rolling off her, but I didn't know what the hell she had to be angry about. If anyone had the right to be angry, it was me. Not her.

She stopped mid-stride down the hallway and turned

toward me with her finger in the air. "You know what?" Then she shook her head and kept walking.

"What, Staci? What could you possibly have to be angry about?"

She pulled her keycard out of her handbag, and I watched her hand shake as she readied it to go in the door.

"You don't think I have a right to be angry? I have every fucking right." She pushed the key in the door and the little lights turned green.

"Then tell me why? Why the hell are you angry?"

"Because." She practically growled before she looked up at me. Really looked at me for the first time since we had been in Vegas, and I could see something inside her breaking.

She took a step toward me, and I let her as she pushed me against the wall right outside her door. She pressed her lips against mine in a rush. Her teeth hit my bottom lip as she desperately clung to me, but I didn't stop her. I let her take what she needed from me. I let her take and take and take until I wasn't sure what I would have left to give her. It was both heaven and hell.

I could taste the liquor on her lips along with her lust. I could taste her need. Her need for me to take away whatever she was feeling. Her need to use me.

"I'm not sleeping with you." I gripped her arms in my hands and gently pushed her away from me.

"What?" She pushed her hair out of her face, and she looked so angry in that moment. I was glad. We could both be angry. "Why not?"

"For one, you're drunk. Two, I'm not going to let you keep using me."

She reared back as if I had slapped her. "Fuck you, Mason."

I advanced on her until her back hit the wall on the opposite side of the hallway. "I would, you know," I whispered against her ear and watched as chill bumps broke out across her skin. "I would fuck you so good if you would stop pushing me away."

She closed her eyes and tried to block out my words, but I leaned closer into her.

"If you just want me to fuck you, then fine. I'll fuck you. But this will be the last time." I could feel my anger for her boiling to the edge. "You can treat me like one of your one-night stands, and this time, I will know the score."

The words tasted disgusting on my lips. I hated them, and I regretted them as soon as I said them.

She was looking up at me, her eyes filled with pain and I couldn't take it anymore. I reached out to touch her, to feel her skin beneath my fingers, and she flinched. She flinched as if I was going to hurt her.

I pulled my hand away from her and searched her eyes. "Staci?"

My voice was broken, as broken as I felt, but I couldn't keep the emotion out of my voice. I couldn't handle the way watching her flinch away from me as if I was some monster made me feel.

"Please, Mason." She wiped a tear from her eye that was just starting to fall.

"I'm sorry." I took a step back from her. "I'm sorry for what I said. I would never hurt you."

She nodded her head, but it was weak and lost. "I know that. I know. I've just had too much to drink, and I need sleep."

"Okay." I took another step away from her and toward my own room.

Whatever Staci was keeping from me and whatever the fuck we were feeling for each other, it was all too much for her. I could see it in her eyes. I could practically feel how tired she was from whatever it was she was going through. So, I didn't push her. Instead, I walked to my room and pulled out my own keycard.

I was one step through the doorway when her voice called out to me.

"Mason." She sounded so weak and so unlike the girl she normally was.

"Yes, Staci."

"Can you just hold me tonight?"

I was back out into the hallway before she could say another word, and I watched tears fill her eyes as I scooped her into my arms and carried her into my room. Neither one of us took off the clothes we were wearing. It wasn't even a thought. I just cradled her against my chest as I climbed into my bed and pulled the blanket over us. My hands held her firmly against me as she cried, and I promised her that I would never let go of her. And I meant every word.

CHAPTER 27

HUNGOVER

STACI

THE POUNDING in my head had been blocking out everything else.

It took me too long to realize that I wasn't in my own room and that the hard surface that was beneath my face was a man who should want absolutely nothing to do with me.

A man who I hurt.

I pressed against his chest and I groaned as I sat up in the bed. Mason's eyes were on me, and it looked like they had probably been on me for a while.

"Morning." His voice was soft as if he could tell how badly I was feeling just by looking at me.

"Morning." My mouth felt like it was stuffed with cotton.

I pressed my hand against my face and tried to think about what to say to him. There were a million things that I needed to say, a million things that he deserved to know, but I didn't know where to start.

His fingers trailed over my face and pushed my hair back, and I braced myself for whatever he was about to say.

"The convention starts at noon. How about you jump in the shower to help you feel better and I'll grab us some coffee?"

I turned to look at him, and he was staring at me without a trace of judgment in his eyes. There was no anger. No hate. His gaze lacked everything that he should have been feeling toward me.

Everything that I deserved.

"And then?" I asked, my voice as rough as I felt.

"And then"—he leaned forward and placed a gentle kiss on my forehead—"we'll talk."

I nodded my head. Even though I knew we had to talk, I knew I couldn't avoid it, I still dreaded it. I dreaded every second of telling him about my past.

The fear of letting him that far in was almost too much to handle.

He climbed out of the bed, still in his clothes from the night before, and he walked to the door. "I'll be back. Okay?"

It was the way his gentle voice spoke to me like I was so fragile I would break that had more tears springing to my eyes as I nodded my head. My heart felt wild with the knowledge of how much he cared about me, of how adamantly he refused to hurt me even though I had hurt him, but it was also breaking under how weak I felt.

When the door closed behind him, I finally moved from the bed and made my way into the bathroom. I took one look in the mirror before I turned away from my mascara stained face. I stripped my clothes from my body, and I stepped under the hot spray of the shower.

The shower smelled like him, the hint of his spicy body wash surrounding me, and I didn't think twice about it when I pulled the bottle off the shelf and squirted it into my hand. I didn't care that I would smell like a man for the rest of the day. It didn't matter. All I could think about was how the smell of him wrapped around me made me feel safe, and if he, if he chose not to want to be anything to me after he found out the secrets I had been keeping, I would need that small comfort.

I scrubbed my face as the hot water cascaded over me, and I took a deep breath, trying to steel my nerves.

The water dripped softly from the faucet as I turned the handle off, and it was the only sound that echoed throughout the steamy bathroom besides my breathing. I wrapped the large fluffy robe around my body before I tied my hair up in a towel, and I reached for the door handle with a trembling hand.

Mason was sitting in a chair by the window with his hands around a coffee cup and his head facing the ceiling, but his gaze darted to mine when I finally walked out of the bathroom.

Neither one of us said a word as I took a seat in the chair next to him and took the coffee that he extended toward me.

I took a long drink before I curled my feet under me in the chair and turned toward him.

He was watching me, waiting for me, giving me time to gather my thoughts, and it hit me in that moment how much more Mason deserved. He deserved far better than I could give him. Far better than me.

"I'm sorry." They were the first words that came out of my mouth without me even thinking, and I was. God, I was so sorry.

"I'm sorry too."

I shook my head at his words. "You have nothing to be sorry about."

"Then just tell me what I did." He looked so desperate in that moment, desperate for the answers I had been keeping from him, desperate for me.

"You didn't do anything, Mason." I set my coffee down on the small table and wrung my hands together.

"I had to do something. Everything was fine then I fucked up somehow."

"I'm the one who is fucked up." I looked him in the eyes, and he closed his mouth with whatever words he was about to say still on his tongue. "I should have never let things get this far without telling you the truth. I was lying to myself thinking that I could get away with what we've been doing without hurting you. I was lying to you."

He didn't say another word. He just leaned back in his chair and watched me.

"Mason," I took a deep breath. "I'm married."

His body physically reared back an inch. "You're what?"

"I'm married." His eyes slammed closed against my words. "That's why I had to go home to Oklahoma. I had to finalize my divorce."

His eyes popped back open, and he stared at me with fire in his gaze. "And is it final?"

"It should be any day now." My lawyer promised me that she would make sure everything went through as quickly as she could get it to, but I still hadn't heard back from her that it was done.

"Why didn't you tell me?" I could see the anger starting to fill him, anger that he had every right to feel. "Do Livy and Parker know?" That thought only seemed to anger him more.

"No." I shook my head. "No one knows. I think Parker has his own guesses about what has been going on with me, but I never told him."

He stood up and ran his fingers through his hair.

"Why? Why would you hide that from me? From everyone?"

He paced through the room and I curled my legs against my chest and wrapped my arms around them.

"It's not something I'm proud of, Mason. It's not something I want to think about."

"How old were you when you got married?" He leaned against the armoire with his arms crossed.

"Eighteen."

He nodded his head. "So, you've been married for six years, but you didn't think it was important to tell me? To tell your friends?"

I opened my mouth to speak, but he kept going. "How does your husband feel about you fucking other men while you're still married?"

Even though I knew he was hurt, I knew that he was speaking to me out of pain, I still felt my temper flaring at his words.

"He doesn't get to feel anything about it." My voice was low, and I tried to control the venom in it.

"So, what? You decided you didn't want to be with him anymore then he didn't get a say about anything. That sounds familiar."

His harsh eyes were so unforgiving.

"That's not fair." I tugged my robe tighter around me.

"Isn't it?" He pushed off the armoire and took a step toward me. "What's not fair about it? The fact that it's the truth or that you don't want to hear it?"

"He didn't get a say in anything anymore because he didn't know where I was."

"You ran?" His voice was almost condescending, and I hated it. I hated that I had put us in this position.

"Yes. I ran. I ran away from our marriage. I ran away from my life in Oklahoma. I ran away from it all."

His steps faltered, and I could practically see the thoughts that were running through his head. Thoughts I never wanted him to have.

"Did he hurt you?"

I closed my eyes against his words, and I cursed myself when I couldn't stop tears from forming in my eyes.

"I'm not him."

"I know that." I couldn't keep my voice from cracking, and it felt like something deeper was cracking with it.

Mason dropped to his knees in front of my chair and wrapped his arms around my stomach. I could feel him trembling with anger or sadness, I wasn't sure, but it still shook me to my core.

"Mason," I whispered his name, but I didn't know what else to say. I didn't know what I needed to do.

"No." He shook his head and reached up to grip my face in his hand. "You don't have to say anything, Staci. You don't owe me anything."

"But I do."

He shook his head again, but he was wrong. He was so wrong.

"Mason, I should have told you. I should have told you before I ever let you develop feelings for me."

"Do you really think it would have made a difference?" He rubbed his thumb over my trembling bottom lip.

"I have baggage, Mason. Too much baggage. I don't expect you to—"

"What? What don't you expect of me?" He leaned closer into me. "Do you expect me to just walk away from you? Do you think that I could do that even if I wanted to?"

I could taste salt on my lips, but Mason's fingers caught my tears and wiped them from my face.

"You deserve better, Mason."

"Don't say that shit." He gripped my chin in his hand and forced me to look at him. "It doesn't matter what you've been through, Staci. I want you."

"I want you too."

Mason's lips were on mine before the last word left my mouth. His touch was unbelievably tender but more potent than anything I had ever felt. He kept his hands on my jaw as he gently kissed me. His lips touched every inch of my face. He pressed his lips against my eyelids. They were a ghost of a touch along my cheek.

A whimper escaped me as he ever so softly sucked my bottom lip into his mouth, and he hesitated when I pressed my body farther into his.

But I needed more of him.

"Please, Mason," I cried out when he held me at a distance.

"We don't have to do this." His voice was rough, and it caused chill bumps to break out across my skin. "Just let me love you."

It was more than I could take, more than I was willing to face in that moment, but God, I was dying for him to.

I pushed my body closer to him again, and Mason stood, leaving me in the chair alone. He gently pulled the towel from my head, letting my mess of wet hair fall around me before he reached down and slowly untied my robe.

It was the first time in what felt like my entire life that I felt naked in front of someone. Truly naked with absolutely nothing between us. No secrets. No lies. No false promises.

It was just us, Mason and I, and when he stared down at my body and took a deep breath, I finally let go of the one I had been holding.

Mason bent at the waist before he gathered me in his arms and carried me to the bed. I was lying on my back with my hair soaking through the white sheets, and I couldn't take my eyes off him.

He took his time as he unbuttoned his shirt one excruci-ating button after another, and I was practically squirming on the bed when he finally pulled his black belt from his pants. When he was completely naked in front of me, he dropped a knee to the mattress and moved over my body without touching me. I could feel the warmth of him above me. My body was begging for me to get closer to him.

He pushed my hair out of my face as he settled on his elbows near my head, and I almost looked away when I saw the look in his eyes. A look that I had been scared of for so long.

He pressed his lips to my forehead before he moved down my body at an achingly slow pace. This wasn't about our bodies. It wasn't about chasing that high of an orgasm. This was more. It was always more, but this was different than anything I had ever felt before.

Mason's body pressed against mine, and it was only moments before he was pushing himself into me. I moaned as he buried his face in my neck, and I reached out for him, for something to hold on to.

His body wasn't rushed as he moved against me, and I could feel my orgasm building. A steady and lethal storm that was brewing inside of me.

Mason's hand roamed over my face as he stared down at me, and I couldn't take my eyes off his. It was more intimate than I had ever been with anyone else, even Ben, but I refused to let myself look away from him. I refused to run from him just because I was scared.

His hips rolled against mine, and I cried out as pleasure shot through my body. It was the kind of pleasure that was all-consuming, the kind that made you lose every ounce of worry or inhibition that you had left.

And when the words slipped past my lips, I blamed it on that pleasure. I blamed it on Mason and everything he was forcing me to feel, but I didn't regret them.

I would never regret them because they were true.

When Mason whispered the same words in my ear, my fingers dug into his back and I let go of every bit of control I was clinging to.

"I love you."

CHAPTER 28

TEAM MACI

MASON

I HAD no interest in going to the damn convention. Especially not after I finally got Staci in my arms. Not after she had finally opened up to me.

I needed to get a handle on the fury that was running through me. As soon as I saw her face when I asked her if he had hurt her, a rage that I had never experienced before ran through my blood. But I had to keep it under control. I wouldn't let her see how angry I was. I didn't want to scare her.

Because I was mad enough to kill.

If I ever did see that motherfucker, I would kill him. Her husband. God, she had a husband. Just that thought alone made me want to murder him. He was supposed to be her everything, but he wasn't. Thank fuck he wasn't, but it didn't make me hate him any less.

Staci had gone to her room to get ready for the convention, and I had gone to the gym and tried my hardest to work out my anger. I was dripping with sweat by the time I made it back to my room, and I was glad that Staci was already downstairs.

She had been working at the convention for an hour by the

time I finally calmed myself down enough to meet them down there.

I had to fight my way through the crowd to get to their booth. There were people surrounding it in every direction you looked, and I didn't blame them. Staci was up on a platform tattooing on a young woman's back when I finally saw her, and it seemed like every other male in the room had his eyes on her as well.

Her jeans were tight and low on her hips, and she had a black tank top on that was knotted in the back showing off her midriff. Everything inside of me screamed to cover her up. I wanted to cover her up and get every other man's eyes off her.

But I wouldn't be that guy.

Because that guy, he wasn't what Staci needed. Staci was by far one of the most independent women I had ever met, and I now knew that she clung to that independence because of her past.

I would never make her feel like I was taking that away from her.

Would I get jealous? Fuck yes. I was jealous right now, but there was a difference between jealousy and possessiveness. I didn't want to possess Staci. I just wanted to love her.

She pulled her eyes off the woman she was tattooing for only a moment to look up at me before she focused back on her work. A small smile formed on her lips, and I had to fight the urge to grab her in my arms in front of all of these people and kiss the hell out of her.

My sister was working at a table behind the booth selling merchandise and talking to people as they came up. Brandon was near Staci on the platform, and he was tattooing a guy's upper arm while people watching in awe.

"Hey, Mrs. James." I bumped my sister's shoulder. "Where is that husband of yours?"

She grinned, a huge ass grin before she pointed toward the edge of their booth where Parker was talking with a few guys who were as tattooed as he was.

"Mrs. James," Livy murmured her new name as she looked down at the simple diamond on her finger. "That's so weird. Right?"

"I think it's pretty perfect." I found a t-shirt out of the stack in front of me and handed it to her. She handed it to the guy in front of her before taking his money then she turned to look at me.

"It is. Isn't it?"

She looked so happy, so insanely happy, and I was beyond relieved that she had found that. That she and Parker had found that in each other after everything they had been through.

"What's the plan for the honeymoon?" My eyes darted back to where Staci was still working.

"When you all head back home tomorrow, we're heading to Hawaii." She did a little luau dance and I chuckled. "I'm going to come home tan and completely relaxed, and you all are going to be insanely jealous."

"You better wear sunscreen. You know how you burn in Tennessee and the sun is different in Hawaii."

"Thank you, Dad." She rolled her eyes, but I pulled her toward me and wrapped my arms around her.

"I'm happy for you, Liv." I looked down at my baby sister, the girl I had been looking out for my entire life, and I thanked God for her.

"I'm happy for you too." She squeezed my shoulder and her eyes traveled to Staci. "She seemed like she was in a much happier mood today."

"I want to make her happy." I watched as Staci laughed at something the woman she was tattooing said then she started bouncing her head to the music that blared through the convention space.

"I know you do." Livy squeezed my arm. "Both of you deserve to be happy."

She was right. We did deserve to be happy, but I only wanted it with Staci. I could only see it with her.

Staci looked up from her work again, her eyes going to where I had stood moments earlier, then she quickly moved her gaze through the crowd until she finally reached Livy and I. She smiled, at me or Livy I wasn't sure, but it was breathtaking nonetheless.

"I didn't really have faith that you could pull this off."

My sister's words pulled my attention away from Staci and back to her. She was still looking toward her best friend.

"You didn't have faith in team Maci?" I poked my finger into her ribs and she laughed.

"I didn't say that. I said I didn't have faith in you. Me being on your team was your saving grace."

I rolled my eyes, and she patted me on my back.

"I need you to man the table for a minute." She pointed to the long line of people that still surrounded their booth. "I need to go kiss my husband."

CHAPTER 29

POWER TOOLS

STACI

I WAS SO DAMN TIRED. The convention had lasted hours after hours, and even though I was incredibly humbled by the amount of support and admiration our little shop was shown, I had wanted nothing more than to crawl into my bed.

So that was what I did. I crawled into my bed with Mason wrapped around me, and we slept until the most annoying sound of my alarm going off this morning woke us up.

Livy and Parker were already on their way to the airport by the time we rolled out of bed, and even though Livy had told me that she thought she could actually fit me inside her luggage with most of her clothing, she didn't even try. She just rode off into the sunrise with her husband and forgot all about me.

Not that I blamed her.

I was just dreading my flight home. I wouldn't be flying home with Mason and Brandon because I couldn't go back to Tennessee yet. I promised my father that I would come back to Oklahoma for a few days to help him get a few things squared away with the house, and I also had to meet my lawyer to get all of my final divorce papers.

Papers that I couldn't wait to hold in my hands.

Mason wasn't too happy that I wasn't going back to Tennessee with him. Not that he would outright say that. Instead, he pouted a little, and I could tell he was running scenarios in his head to try to talk me out of it.

"How long are you going to be in Oklahoma?" He ran his thumb over the back of my knuckles.

"Just a few days. My dad is working on repairing the old porch around his house, and I promised him that I would help before I head back to Tennessee."

"You do construction?" He cocked an eyebrow at me.

"I'm pretty handy with a power tool. Thank you very much." I shoved his shoulder.

"I could come with you and help. You know handling tools is my specialty."

"Handling your tool or tools that belong to others?" I smirked at him.

"Smartass." He rolled his eyes at me and settled back in the hard airport chair.

"You'd really want to come with me?" I asked. It was probably a stupid idea to even consider, but I had to admit that I wasn't ready to be away from him. I didn't care how weak that made me.

"If you want me to, I do," he said it so casually, but it was a big deal. My father hadn't met anyone from my life in Tennessee. Not because I didn't want him to, but I had always gone home to visit him. He knew all about Parker and Brandon and me working at the shop with them, and I talked his ear off about Livy on the phone, but this was different.

I had told him about Mason while I had been home for the last couple weeks, but my dad was wary of any man at this point. He didn't want me to get hurt again, and if he could help prevent it, he would.

"Are you sure that you're ready to meet my dad?"

"Well," he scratched his beard. "Not when you say it like that."

"It's just that my dad is protective." I took a sip of my warm coffee.

"As he should be."

"And he's big."

"Duly noted." Mason smiled.

"And he owns several guns."

Mason turned toward me. "Are you trying to scare me into not going?"

"No." I shook my head. "I want you to go. I just want you to be prepared. My dad can be a lot to handle."

"You want me to go?" He tucked a piece of hair behind my ear.

"Yes."

"Then I'll go."

And just like that, Mason Connor had slid out of the friend-zone and was on his way to meet my father.

CHAPTER 30

MILE HIGH CLUB

MASON

I'D BE LYING if I said I wasn't scared shitless about meeting Staci's father.

I wasn't scared of the man himself per se, but I was scared of what he would think about me. Of what he would think about mine and Staci's relationship. Because I didn't even know where we stood exactly.

I guess that was what scared me the most.

I didn't think twice about switching my ticket and climbing onto the airplane with her. I just climbed into the seat next to her and held her hand through takeoff.

We were both exhausted, her more so than me after all the work she did yesterday, and I wasn't surprised when she leaned her head against my shoulder and fell asleep as soon as we were in the air.

But if she didn't move soon, I was going to pee on myself. After about an hour and a half into the flight, Staci shifted enough that I could pull my arm out from beneath her without waking her up. I quickly unlatched my seatbelt and made my way down the plane to the bathroom.

A flight attendant was coming down the aisle at the same time, and we barely managed to squeeze past each other without me bumping into an old lady in her seat.

I quietly apologized since her husband was asleep next to her, and she smiled up at me and patted my arm.

Finally, I made it to the bathroom. I splashed water on my face to wake me up. Staci had slept curled against my body last night, and even though it felt amazing, I kept waking up every few hours to make sure she was still there.

I had to make sure I wasn't dreaming.

I pushed the lock and pulled the tiny door open, and it almost hit me in the face with the force of someone coming through it.

"What the fuck?" I said before I recognized her black hair and heard her soft giggle.

"What are you doing?" I whispered as she closed the door behind her. The bathroom was so small that neither one of us could really move with the other one in there.

"The movie theatre. Really, Mason?" She pulled her t-shirt over her head.

"What?" I chuckled as I watched her.

"You said that the movie theatre was the craziest place you've ever had sex." She popped the button of her jeans. "That's pathetic really."

"So, what?" I started undoing my belt. "You're here to help me up my game?"

"Exactly." She pulled her jeans down her legs. "What kind of girl do you take me for?"

She laughed as I gripped my hands under her ass and lifted her to the almost nonexistent bathroom sink. "A very, very bad girl."

She smirked and I pulled my jeans down my hips.

"You mean I haven't ruined my bad girl persona with you?"

I stepped toward her and she wrapped her fingers around my cock before she slid it up and down her wetness. I could barely form a thought.

"No." I lined myself up with her and thrust into her as I spoke through gritted teeth. "I still think you're a bad girl. You're just a bad girl who has fallen a bit."

Her head slammed back against the bathroom mirror as I pulled out then thrust into her again. "And where exactly do you think I've fallen?"

I caressed her breast through the thin layer of her bra and felt her nipple peak beneath my touch.

"Into me."

Her eyes met mine and they were on fire. "You think you're the one to tame the bad girl?" Her pussy convulsed around me, and she gripped her fingers in her hair and arched her back as a moan escaped her lips.

"No." I shook my head, but she couldn't see me with her head thrown back in pleasure. "I'm just the one who gets to keep her."

She fell apart around me then, her body milking out every drop of my own pleasure, and I had to press my hand against her mouth to muffle her screams. She may have come into this bathroom willingly, but I didn't think she really wanted to get caught. The last thing we needed was to get in trouble by some air official.

She bit down on my hand before she ran over the skin with her tongue, and I came with a loud moan as I buried my face in her shoulder.

She pressed her lips against mine, a tender kiss, before we started banging into things as we tried to quickly get dressed.

"Quit laughing," I told her on a chuckle. "You're going to get us caught."

"We're not going to get caught." She rolled her beautiful

eyes at me. "I'll go out first then you come out a minute or so later. No one will think a thing."

"Uh huh." I buckled my belt and slid it into place.

"Trust me. I'm like a ninja." She grinned as she opened the door and almost ran into one of the flight attendants.

She was an older lady who looked all business, and I braced myself when she looked into the small bathroom at the two of us. "I hope the two of you had fun. Now get back to your seats. We're going to be landing soon."

"Yes, ma'am," Staci called after the flight attendant as she started walking away.

I bumped into her shoulder and she looked back at me.

"Yes, ma'am?" I cocked an eyebrow. "What a badass you are."

"Shut up." She rolled her eyes again, and I followed her back to our seats.

I glanced over at the older woman I almost ran into earlier as I took my seat, and she was still smiling at me. "Oh, to be young again." She laughed and Staci, my little bad girl, buried her face in my chest.

CHAPTER 31

MEETING THE FAMILY

STACI

THIS WAS GOING to be a disaster.

I just knew it.

Me and Mason weren't ready for him to meet my father. I don't know what the hell I was thinking.

I was going to regret this decision.

"Dad." I pushed the front door open and turned back to look at Mason who was carrying all of our bags. "We're here."

I could hear the creak of his old recliner and he appeared around the corner only a moment later.

"Well, how was it?" The sound of his deep voice instantly relaxed me just a bit, and I moved into his arms when he held them out for me.

"It was good," I mumbled against his chest. "We were super busy."

My dad let me out of his hug, but he kept an arm slung over my shoulders. "You must be this Mason that I keep hearing so much about."

I pinched my dad on his back to warn him not to embarrass me, but he just smiled harder.

"Yes, sir." Mason held his hand out to my father. "Mason Connor. It's nice to meet you."

"Likewise." My father shook Mason's hand before waving him farther in the house. "Come on in and put those bags down. I know my Staci doesn't pack light."

"No, sir, she doesn't." Mason laughed as he put the bags down where my father showed him.

"What are your plans for today?" My father looked down at me.

"I think we could both use a nap. No plans after that."

"Okay. I'm sure you can manage showing Mason the guest room then." He looked over at Mason to drive his point home.

"Yes, Dad." I gave him a look that begged him to stop, but he only chuckled.

"I'll see you both in a few hours." My dad tussled my hair before he made his way back into the living room.

I showed Mason to the guest room where he put down his bags before he carried my bags into my old bedroom. It was still decorated the way it had been when I moved out at eighteen years old, and I watched as Mason looked around the room taking it all in.

I plopped down on my bed and looked up at Mason. "You could come join me. You know?" I patted the small space that was left on my old twin size bed.

"Not happening." He chuckled and started toward the door.

"I don't even get a kiss?" I pouted, and he ran his fingers through his hair before he made his way over to me.

"One kiss," he murmured as he leaned down and pressed his lips to mine.

They were gone far too quickly.

"That's it?" I leaned up on my elbows.

"I'll see you after our nap." Mason walked to the door and held the handle in his hand.

"We're not even going to mess around in my old bedroom?" I whispered.

"No." Mason shook his head and laughed. "I'm pretty sure your dad has already thought of a thousand ways he could kill me."

"That's probably true." I dropped back down on my bed.

Mason's laugh echoed through the hallway as he left my room.

...

I felt like I had been asleep for hours.

One look out my dark bedroom window insured me that I had.

I made my way to the guest room to wake up Mason, but he was nowhere to be seen. The bed didn't look like he had ever even laid in it.

The house was quiet as I walked through it, and no one answered me as I called out for my dad and Mason. I could hear laughter coming from outside, and I pushed open the old creaky screen door to find my dad and Mason sitting on the porch with a beer in their hands.

"Hello there, sleepy head." My dad chuckled.

"Hey." I stretched my arms over my head and looked around the porch. "Did you all already fix the porch?"

I could see new boards where the old, rotten ones had been, and it looked amazing.

"Yeah. Mason here is pretty damn handy."

"Is he now?"

Mason looked so cocky as he smiled up at me.

"He helped me fix the porch, and we fixed that leaning fence post too."

Mason's smirk only got bigger.

"Suck up."

My dad laughed. "Don't be running him off now. I think I like this one."

"You just met him, Dad. Don't be giving him your blessing after one afternoon together."

"Has she always been this dramatic?" Mason asked my father, but he was still looking at me.

"Since the day she was born." My dad shook his head. "She's always been stubborn as hell too."

"Dad," I groaned.

"What? You have." He ran his hand over his salt and pepper hair that was once as black as mine.

"You both frustrate the hell out of me." I opened the screen door to walk back inside, and my dad's voice called out behind me.

"That's a good sign you know."

CHAPTER 32

NOT ANYMORE

MASON

WE HAD BEEN WALKING around her small town for the last hour or so, and she was pointing out everything she used to do and all the places she used to hang out.

But she never talked about her ex-husband. It was as if she had tried to remove all memories of him from this town and from her mind.

Her dad and I had hit it off as soon as I walked back into the living room and offered to help him with his porch. He threatened me right before we got started. He gave me a speech about never hurting his girl, and when I told him that I would do everything within my power to make sure she was never hurt again, I felt like he believed me.

Because it was the truth.

I never wanted to see that look in her eyes that she had in Vegas. I refused to ever cause it.

"This is where I first took art lessons." She pointed to a small building that looked like it at seen better days.

"Yeah?"

"Yeah. My drawings were bad though. So bad." She winced.

"I don't believe you." I gripped her hand in mine and she slowly laced her fingers with mine.

"Trust me. It was bad."

"I can't imagine you ever being bad. My tattoo is perfect, and I didn't even tell you what I wanted. You don't just learn that kind of talent."

She smiled but didn't respond.

"Do you miss being here?"

"Yes and no." She looked around at the town she had run away from. "I miss my dad. It feels like home when I go to his house, but the rest of this"—she motioned her hand around us —"it's not home to me."

"Where is home to you?"

Her eyes met mine. "The shop. I feel more at home there than I do anywhere else. Even my apartment."

I could completely understand that. Sometimes I felt more at home when I was at work then I did when I came home to an empty house.

"Why haven't you bought a house yet? You told me all your big dreams of what your house would look like. What's been holding you back?" I could see the pain in her eyes at my question, and I hated that I had even brought it up.

"Ben." Her hand tightened in mine slightly. "That's his name." She took a deep breath. "I didn't want to do anything that he could take from me. I didn't want to give him an opportunity to ruin my life again."

I took in her words and they filled me with anger. "You've been living with one foot constantly out the door."

The look on her face told me that she was just now realizing that herself. "Yeah. I guess I have been."

I tugged her hand to stop her and pulled her flush with my body. "Not anymore."

She was staring up into my eyes, and there was so much vulnerability there, but there was also strength. "Not anymore," she repeated my words, and I leaned down and tasted them on her lips.

CHAPTER 33

TACO TUESDAY

STACI

"HOW LONG DO I have to deal with you in the honeymoon phase? It's starting to get annoying."

I looked over at my best friend and flipped her off.

"You're the one who literally just got back from your honeymoon. Not me."

"I know." She plopped down in my tattoo chair. "But ever since you and Mason have been back from your dad's house, I can barely stand to be around either one of you."

"You're being ridiculous." I opened one of my drawers and pulled out some supplies.

"Am I?" She tapped her chin. "Last night at dinner you barely even spoke to me. You were too busy talking about what you and Mason did or what you and Mason had planned."

"Are you jealous?" I looked at her out of the corner of my eye.

"Of course, I'm not jealous. I could never be jealous of Mason, but you are my best friend."

She actually crossed her arms and I couldn't help but laugh at her pouting.

"How do you think he felt when you started dating Parker?"

"And now you're defending him!"

"I am not." I moved over in front of her and pulled her into my arms. "I never realized you were such a needy best friend."

"Well, I am," she mumbled into my chest.

"Then let's go." I tugged on her hand and she looked up at me.

"Go where?"

"It's Taco Tuesday. I'm sure we can find somewhere to serve us some margaritas."

"What about the guys?" she asked hesitantly, and I wanted to point out to her that she was far more wrapped in Parker than I was Mason. At least that's what I was claiming.

"They can hang out on their own for one night." I grabbed my cell phone off my table and tucked it into my back pocket. "Are you coming or what?"

"Yes. I'm coming. Don't get your panties in a wad." She reached her hand out, and I started to pull her out of the chair before she got sassy. "You really are spending too much time with my brother."

"Hey, Livy."

"What?" She pushed against the arms of the chairs when she realized I wasn't going to help her up.

"The first night I had sex with your brother was in that chair."

"Gross." She jumped out of the chair as if it now carried an STD. "You are such an asshole."

"Yes." I looped my arm in hers. "But I'm your asshole."

CHAPTER 34

TRASHED

MASON

I KNEW when Staci text me that she and Livy were going out for margaritas that it wasn't a good idea, but I didn't realize how bad until I heard their laughter before I even managed to get through the front door of the restaurant.

They were trashed.

Staci was wearing a sombrero on her head, and my sister was practically lying in the booth she was in laughing. There were only two margarita glasses on their table, not a damn trace of food, but there were two pitchers that had nothing but ice left in them.

"Are you two having fun?"

They both looked up at me like two deer in headlights then they broke out in a fit of giggles.

"You are so handsome," Staci said the words through her laughter and Livy scrunched up her nose.

"That's so gross. That's my brother."

"I know." Staci nodded her head and that damn sombrero bounced back and forth. "But look at him."

Livy closed one eye and stared up at me. "Nope." She

popped the p so loudly that most of the restaurant turned to look. "I don't see it."

"Okay." I looked down at them. "It's time to go. Have you all paid your bill yet?"

"Nope." My sister said the word again, and they both broke out in more hysterics.

"Don't move."

Livy was still looking at me with one eye closed, but Staci saluted me.

I went to the counter and paid their ridiculous bill that proved that they had drunk far too many margaritas before I made my way back to their table. It took me forever to get them out to my truck. Not only could they not walk straight, but they wouldn't stop laughing long enough to focus.

It took about every ounce of strength and patience I had to get them in the backseat. They were leaning against one another, their hair was a mess, and they were holding each other's hands.

I text Parker before I pulled out of the driveway and told him to be outside to get his wife when I pulled up.

"I love you, Livy." Staci's voice was so soft I could barely hear it.

"I love you too. You're my sister." Livy hiccupped, and I prayed that she didn't throw up in my truck.

"What if we actually become sisters?" Staci whispered, and my heart thundered in my chest.

"Like sisters-in-law?" Livy asked then the two of them started laughing again. "I can't wait for you all to get married."

"Shhh, Livy." I saw Staci slam her hand over Livy's mouth, and I tried to hide my laugh. "He's right there."

"What does it matter?" Livy's mumbled voice was barely understandable. "He already knows you love him."

Staci groaned then they were quiet for the next several minutes.

When I finally pulled up outside Parker and Livy's house, they were both passed out against each other and Livy was letting out the tiniest little snore.

"It looks like they had fun." Parker opened my back door and lifted Livy in his arms.

"That would be an understatement." I chuckled as I ran my fingers through my hair.

He nodded toward Staci who was completely sprawled out in the backseat. "You got her?"

I knew he meant did I have her tonight, but I had her. I had her for everything she needed. "I got her."

He nodded his head as if he understood exactly what I meant, then he carried my drunk ass sister into their house.

CHAPTER 35

HOME

STACI

Two Months Later

I WAS RUNNING LATE for dinner at Mason's house, but work was crazy. The guy I had been tattooing was not prepared for the commitment he was making when he asked for a full sleeve, and I dreaded having to listen to him bitch through the whole thing during his next session.

I had tattooed eighteen-year-old girls who had handled it better.

He caused me to have a damn headache.

"I'm here. I'm here," I yelled through the house as I threw my bag down on the table in the living room and moved toward the kitchen.

I almost tripped when I saw the kitchen covered in yellow daisies. My favorite, yellow daisies.

"What's going on?" I looked at Mason who was leaning against the kitchen counter with a smile on his face.

"Do you like it here?" He didn't move an inch from where he stood.

"What?" I was so confused.

"Do you like it here? My house? Do you feel at home here?"

I looked around at his house, a house that I had been spending more nights at than my own apartment and turned back to him.

"Of course, I do."

"But do you really feel at home here?" He took a step toward me and my breath caught in my throat.

"Yes." I touched one of the yellow daisies. "Why are you asking me that?"

"Because." He moved another step closer to me and wrapped his arms around my center. "I think it's time that you start living with both feet on the ground."

I didn't know what to say to him. I didn't know what he was asking of me.

"My house." He motioned around him. "This place. It means nothing without you. It doesn't feel like a home without you." He ran his fingers along my cheek. "I know that it takes a lot for you to trust, but I want you to put your trust in me. I want you to trust that I will always put you first and I will always take care of you. I want you to trust that as long as you're willing to take a chance on me, I will want you."

"I do." I could barely get out the words.

"Then move in with me."

It may not have seemed like much to some, but it was everything to me. It was everything that he knew what it meant to me. It had been so long since I had truly felt at home, and he was right. It didn't matter where we were. I wouldn't feel at home anywhere without him. He had become my home. My safe place.

"Are you sure?" I didn't want to push him into anything. I didn't want him to feel like he had to do this.

"I've never been more sure about anything." He pushed a piece of hair out of my face, and I rose on my tiptoes to press my mouth to his.

My hands roamed over his beard, and I kissed him hard.

"Is that a yes?" He mumbled against my lips.

I laughed and nodded over and over again as he slid his arms around me and lifted me off the ground.

"Finn's excited."

"He is?" I looked out the window toward his house.

"Yeah. He told me that he could definitely get you to be his girlfriend now that you were his neighbor."

"And what did you tell him?" He ran his fingers over the back of my neck as he looked down at me.

"I told him that if he wanted to stay best friends, then he needed to back off my girl."

I pressed my lips together to stop my laughter.

"That little shit told me that he could find more best friends, but he'd never find another girl like you."

I couldn't control my laughter then, and Mason pinched my side which only made me laugh harder.

I watched his eyes dance with humor before he started carrying me toward the bedroom. Our bedroom.

"It looks like I taught him something right after all."

He smiled then leaned down and pressed his lips against mine.

He tossed me onto the bed, and I laughed as I looked at the man that I loved.

And I knew that I could read every romance novel that lined the walls of my apartment, but nothing would ever compare to this.

Because Mason Connor had somehow surpassed every single one of my book boyfriends.

THE END

OTHER BOOKS BY HOLLY RENEE:

I hope you enjoyed Where Bad Girls Go to Fall with Staci and Mason ! If you want more from their world, keep reading for the synopsis of Staci's and Brandon's stories, Where Good Girls Go to Die and Where Bad Boys are Ruined.

WHERE GOOD GIRLS GO TO DIE

THE GOOD GIRLS SERIES, BOOK 1

A Second Chance Romance

It was a bad idea from the beginning.

He was my brother's best friend and the definition of unavailable.

But I didn't care. I had loved him for as long as I could remember.

He was worth the risk. He was worth everything.

But then he broke my heart as easily as I fell for him.

He watched me fall, spiraling out of control, and as I reached for him, he wasn't there to catch me.

So I ran.

Four years later, I never expected to see him again.

He was still my brother's best friend, and he was more unavailable than ever.

He looked every bit the bad boy I knew he was, covered in tattoos and a crooked smile.

Guarding my heart from him was top priority because Parker James was where good girls go to die.

Unfortunately for him, I wasn't a good girl anymore.

WHERE BAD BOYS ARE RUINED

THE GOOD GIRLS SERIES, BOOK 3

A Good Girl/ Bad Boy Romance

I ate leftover cupcakes and cracked macarons for breakfast.

I was ninety percent sure he simply ate up girls like me.

I was covered in paint splatters, cake batter, and sweat the first time I met him.

He was covered in badass tattoos and a smile that seemed to hold a secret I would never figure out.

Rule number 1 was never, under any circumstances, fall for the man who I wrote my lease check to.

So, I tucked him away in the "Fantasize Only" compartment of my brain and called it a day.

But he didn't make it easy.

He was arrogant, funny, and the biggest flirt I had ever met.

Most of the time, I didn't know if I was just a game to him.

If I didn't know better, I'd say he was on a mission to ruin my life.

And maybe my heart, too.

THE WRONG PRINCE CHARMING

A College Romance

EVERY LITTLE GIRL dreams of being swept off her feet by a charming Prince.

But my life was no fairy tale.

And in this kingdom called college, the rules went out the window.

I'd known golden boy, Theo Hunt, was the one for me since we were kids. My heart was his for the taking, but I had become nothing more than the MVP of the campus king's friend-zone.

Easton Cole was a storm I couldn't have predicted. He knocked me off my feet and stole my heart. But he was off limits. Not only was he was Theo's frat brother, but he was the teacher's assistant in English 101 and I was acing every test.

My heart was torn, my feelings tangled.

Because as soon as I noticed Easton, Theo finally noticed me.

I was in love with two guys, as different as night and day, but I could only have one.

I only hoped I didn't choose The Wrong Prince Charming.

BOTTOMS UP

THE ROCK BOTTOM SERIES, BOOK 1

A Friends to Lovers Romance

From the moment I met him, I knew he was trouble.

He was reckless, cocky, and everything I shouldn't want.

I had a life all figured out, and Tucker Moore was not a part of the plan.

But somehow I slipped.

One moment I had it all under control.

The next I was spiraling around him, begging him for whatever he would give me.

But as quickly as I fell for him, it all crumbled around us.

Because everything I thought I knew was far from the truth.

There was only one way to fix what we had done.

So I turned my world Bottoms Up.

DOUBLE SHOT

A Sexy Office Romance

HOW DO you screw up your life in three steps? Easy.

Step one: Graduate from college with no prospective jobs lined up.

Step two: Move back home with your parents because no job unfortunately equals no money.

Step three: Forget to Facebook stalk the guy who broke your heart before accepting a job in a town that has a smaller population than a frat party on a Wednesday night.

I could quit but living with my parents forever didn't seem like a solid life plan.

Jase Hale was the golden boy. Our boss thought he was beyond talented. The receptionist sent him more flirty smiles and baked goods than was considered normal for a woman old enough to be his mom.

I tried to avoid him and his undeniable charm at all costs.

He did everything he could to get under my skin.

Every encounter left me reeling.

Every smirk made my stomach flip.

I assumed he was playing with me, just pushing my buttons like always, but when he lifted me onto my desk and shut me up with his lips on mine, I was more confused than ever.

It didn't matter that he was trying to prove me wrong. Having my heart broken by the same jerk twice in one lifetime wasn't an option.

He only got one shot with me and he sure as hell didn't order a double.

STAY UP TO DATE ON FUTURE
RELEASES!

**Click this link to sign up for the Holly Renee
Mailing List:
Newsletter**

Stay connected with Holly Renee:

Facebook

Instagram

ACKNOWLEDGMENTS

To my husband, Hubie: You always support me, even when you have to sacrifice more than you ever should. I couldn't do any of this without you. I would have given up long ago if it wasn't you who had my back. Thank you. Thank you for believing in me. Thank you for believing in my dreams. I love you.

To my mom and my sisters: I may be the Mouth from the South, but you three are the best group of cheerleaders a girl could ask for.

To Cheryl Woods-Lucero: Thank you for always taking the smallest pieces of my stories and helping me every step of the way. I can't tell you what your help and support means to me.

To you, Reader: Thank you for taking a chance on my story. I can't express how much it means to me.

xo, Holly